The Amara Necklace

K J Godsey

Spanish Peaks Publishing

Copyright © 2024 by K J Godsey

All rights reserved.

No portion of this book may be reproduced in any form without written permission from the publisher or author, except as permitted by U.S. copyright law.

"To my daughter Catalina, my inspiration for this book. Your creativity and spirit remind me that every adventure is filled with wonder. This story is for you. May your imagination always lead you to new discoveries."

Acknowledgements

As I sit down to write this, the acknowledgement page of my very first novel, I am filled with gratitude for the people who encouraged me to bring this story to life. To my children Colton, Aidan, Blake, Catalina, and Sofia—thank you. Your unwavering support and belief in me, even when I doubted myself, kept me going. I've dreamed of putting pen to paper for a very long time, but it's your encouragement that gave me the courage to finally do it. Hopefully, I will succeed in my mission of writing a book for each of you. To my mother, your review of the manuscript was like winds to my sail. Making me feel like the story might actually be good.

Writing a novel is a journey, and like any adventure, it's bound to have its bumps along the way. I've poured my thoughts into every page, yet as a first-time author, I know there will be moments that don't quite hit the mark or details that could be smoother. Not to mention spelling errors. I ask for your patience and understanding in those moments and hope that, despite any imperfections, you'll enjoy the story within these pages as much as I enjoyed writing it. Each character has become like a real person to me, and every chapter represents countless hours of revision, and sometimes complete rewrites. If one plot hole is plugged, it opens up three more in previous chapters.

To my wonderful wife Barbara, thank you for letting me get lost in this world and for cheering me on as I found my way through it. Your understanding when I missed family movie nights, staying up until the wee hours of the morning, and your excited face when I emerged from my office with a new chapter to share made all the difference. Your fingerprints are on these pages in ways you might not even realize, from casual conversations that sparked ideas to the personalities that influenced my characters. Those late-night consults when writer's block seemed insurmountable and the countless cups of coffee I drank as I ran holes in the story by you. Those discussions meant more than you'll ever know.

Here's to the start of a new chapter, and I'm grateful to have you along for the ride. Whether this book finds its way to bestseller lists or simply put on a shelf to never be read, I know that the journey of writing it has already changed my life in ways I didn't expect. I hope these words bring you joy and inspire you to embark on your own path.

The Amara Necklace

Chapter One

Cat sneezed as another cloud of dust billowed up from the box she'd just opened, tickling her nose and making her eyes water. The attic of her grandmother's manor was a treasure trove of forgotten memories, each item a potential story waiting to be unearthed, its secrets longing to be discovered after years of silent slumber. Catalina had lived at the Hawthorn Manor with her parents until a few years ago, when her parents decided to move south for her father's job. Now it's just her summer retreat when she spends time with her grandmother. This is where she loved to be, with its sprawling grounds, along with her childhood friends that still lived in the area.

"You alright up there, sweetie?" Evelyn's voice drifted up from the bottom of the stairs, concern evident in her tone.

"Fine, Grandma!" Cat called back, waving away the dust with a flick of her wrist. "This dust is making me sneeze. Nothing I can't handle!"

The attic was a place of wonder to Cat. She'd often rummage around her old boxes. Today, Cat and her grandmother had decided to gather a few old items to donate to the local chapter of the Salvation Army.

She turned back to the task at hand, carefully lifting out old photo albums bound in cracked leather and what looked like a stack of yellowed letters, their edges dried and delicate. As she set them aside with care, something caught her eye at the bottom of the box. A glint of white peeked out from a half open wooden box beneath a faded silk scarf, its shimmering presence impossible to ignore.

Cat's heart quickened, a surge of excitement coursing through her veins. She gently pushed aside the fabric, her fingers trembling slightly as they revealed a stunning necklace. The chain was intricately woven, a delicate clasp of metal holding a sapphire pendant adorned with other deep blue stones surrounded by diamonds that seemed to shimmer and pulse with a reflective light, even in the dim attic light.

"Whoa," she breathed, lifting the necklace from its resting place with a sense of awe. It felt heavy in her hands, the weight of its history pressing against her palms like it contained its own force of gravity. The craftsmanship was exquisite, unlike anything she'd seen before, each detail speaking of a master's touch.

Cat's mind raced, questions tumbling over one another in her thoughts. Why had she never seen this before? Why was it hidden away up here in this dusty attic instead of proudly displayed in her grandmother's jewelry box downstairs? Has this been misplaced or lost?

"Grandma?" she called out, unable to keep the excitement from her voice, which quivered with anticipation. "I think I found something you might want to see! It's incredible!"

She heard the creak of the stairs as Evie made her way up to the landing of the attic, each step slow and measured. Cat turned, holding the necklace up to catch the light streaming through the dusty window, watching as it cast reflections across the room like a prism.

"Look at this! It's absolutely beautiful. Is it a family heirloom? It looks so old and valuable!"

As Evie reached the top of the stairs, her eyes widened, focusing on the necklace with an intensity that startled Cat. The color drained from her face, leaving her complexion milky white, and for a moment, Cat thought she might faint. She'd never seen her grandmother look so shaken.

"Grandma? Are you okay?" Cat asked, worry creeping into her voice as she took a step towards Evie.

Evie's hand trembled visibly as she reached out towards the necklace, her fingers stopping just short of touching it as if a force field was around the jewel. Her voice, when she finally spoke, was barely above a whisper, filled with a mix of emotions Cat couldn't quite decipher. "Where... where did you find that?"

Cat blinked, surprised by her grandmother's reaction. She gestured towards the open box behind her, its contents spilling out onto the dusty attic floor.

"It was in a box that was in that old chest over there, Grandma. Mixed in with some photo albums and letters." She held the necklace up, its blue stones catching the light. "Isn't it gorgeous? I've never seen anything like it before."

Evie's eyes darted between Cat and the necklace, her expression a mix of fear and something else—regret, perhaps? Her voice came out sharp, almost panicked.

"Put it back, Cat. Right now!"

Cat's excitement stumbled, replaced by confusion. "What? But Grandma—"

"I said put it back!" Evie's tone left no room for argument. She took a step forward, her hands outstretched as if to snatch the necklace away. "That necklace... it's not meant to be out. It needs to stay in that box. Do you understand?"

Cat's grip on the necklace tightened. "But why? What's wrong with it?"

Evie's eyes softened slightly, but the urgency in her voice remained.

"Please, sweetie. Just trust me on this. Put it back in the chest and forget you ever saw it. It's... it's better that way."

Reluctantly and confused, Cat moved towards the chest. She looked down at the necklace one last time, its beauty seeming to mock her as she gently placed it back among the faded photographs and crumbling letters.

"There," she said, unable to keep the disappointment from her voice. "It's back where I found it."

Evie's shoulders sagged with visible relief. She approached the chest, her movements quick despite her age, and closed the lid with a decisive thud.

"Thank you. Now, let's go downstairs. I think we've had enough excitement for one day."

As they descended the creaky attic stairs, Cat couldn't shake the feeling that she'd stumbled upon something far more significant than just an old piece of jewelry. Her grandmother's reaction had been too intense, too fearful for this to be a simple family heirloom.

What secrets was her grandmother hiding? And why was she so determined to keep that beautiful necklace buried in the past?

Cat retreated to her room to ponder her grandmother's response upon discovering the necklace. Following an hour of deep reflection, she decided that maybe a warm cup of tea wasn't a bad idea after all, and perhaps it would help calm her mind. She made her way to the kitchen, craving her favorite, Chamomile tea with a bit of honey. She made her way down the grand staircase onto the ground floor. As she passed the large double doors of the study, Cat's ears perked up at the sound of hushed voices emanating from the library beyond. Her curiosity piqued, she slowed her pace, coming to a silent stop at the entrance of the massive wooden double doors. The intricately carved panels loomed before her, their imposing presence a stark contrast to the secretive whispers within. Unnoticed by those engaged in conversation, Cat pressed herself against the cool wood, her heart quickening as she strained to catch every word. She knew eavesdropping wasn't polite, but the temptation to uncover more of the reason her grandmother was upset was too great to resist. With bated breath, she listened intently, hoping to glean some insight into the web of secrets that seemed to envelop her grandmother and the necklace.

She perceived her grandmother's somewhat shaky voice, tinged with a noticeable tension and unease. The man's voice was unknown to her.

"I've already explained. We mustn't discuss this in her presence. Not at this time. She's unaware of the complete story, and I intend to keep it that way for now." Evelyn said, as a matter of fact.

"However, Evelyn, it's inevitable that she'll uncover the truth. She's no longer a child. What's your strategy when she begins to ask questions? You know she will," a cryptic voice responded in hushed tones, pitched with concern.

"I'll divulge what's necessary—when the moment is appropriate," Evie retorted, her voice firm but tinged with a hint of worry.

"Do you genuinely believe you can conceal it forever? That necklace—it's not merely a family keepsake. There are individuals who still remember. People who think it was... stolen," the unknown man whispered, the word 'stolen' hanging heavily in the air.

Evie inhaled deeply, her voice now a little louder and more firm. "That's inaccurate. You're well aware, that tale is merely... hearsay. We've been through this before."

"Hearsay or not, it's dangerous. What if a certain someone comes searching for it again? What if they discover she knows where it is, or worse, possesses it? Have you considered the consequences?"

"No one will uncover the truth. I've maintained its secrecy for all these years, and I'll keep doing so. I will not allow her to become entangled in this mess," she countered, her voice a mix of determination and fear.

"You can't hide it forever, Evelyn. The truth will surface eventually, regardless of your desires. You must prepare for that eventuality." As the man finished his sentence, Cat heard his firm-soled shoes take a few steps towards the outside entrance of the library.

"This sort of situation doesn't get better with time," he stated matter-of-factly and departed the residence with a gentle thump of the door closing, leaving a heavy silence in his wake.

Cat's thoughts began to swirl, a flood of questions and suspicions. Stolen? What could they mean by 'stolen'? Cat retreated silently from behind the study doors, her pulse quickening, her mind reeling with the implications of what she'd just heard. The exchange had left her with more questions than answers, each new piece of information only serving to deepen the mystery. Could the necklace she'd found in the attic harbor a more sinister history than she knew? The weight of the possibility settled on her shoulders, igniting a fierce determination to uncover the truth, no matter the cost.

Cat quietly and quickly ascended the stairs back to her room, her nimble feet skipping a step with each calculated footing. Her heart raced as she moved, adrenaline coursing through her veins. She reached her sanctuary at the end of the long, rugged hallway and entered swiftly, closing the door with a soft click behind her. The early afternoon sun filtered through the partially drawn curtains, casting long, eerie shadows across the floor, but she barely registered the time of day or the shifting light. Her mind was a whirlwind of activity, frantically replaying the fragments of the hushed conversation she had just overheard. Each word, each tone, each pause seemed to hold a hidden meaning, and Cat was determined to unravel the mystery that had suddenly presented itself.

Cat paced around the room, her thoughts spinning. *Stolen?* The word lingered in her mind like a bad taste. Her grandmother had always spoken about the family heirlooms as something precious, but now it seemed this necklace was cloaked in secrets. And danger.

What are they hiding? She couldn't shake the unease that gnawed at her.

Her gaze landed on the old wooden desk sitting against the wall, a piece that had once belonged to her grandmother before it was passed down to her. It was heavy and worn, its surface scratched from years of use, and the brass handles were tarnished with age, their once-bright finish dulled to a muted patina. The oak wood still held a rich warmth despite its imperfections, each mark and dent telling stories of the generations before her. For as long as she could remember, she'd kept her schoolwork and random bits of her life in there—nothing important. Old homework assignments, half-finished sketches, movie ticket stubs, and birthday cards from years past filled its drawers in organized chaos. She also remembered some of her grandmother's papers were still in the drawer, tucked away in the back corner, where she'd never bothered to look too closely. But now, as she stared at it, something stirred inside her—an inexplicable urge that maybe she'd overlooked something significant all this time.

She walked over to it, her fingers trailing over the worn wood. The thought crept into her mind: *What if there's something here that I've missed?*

Cat opened the top drawer, expecting to see the usual clutter of papers and notebooks. She started rifling through them—old letters, postcards, and birthday cards she'd collected over the years. But nothing stood out. She was about to give up when something strange caught her eye.

The bottom of the drawer didn't look quite right. The wood there was slightly uneven, as if a piece of it was out of place. Her pulse quickened.

Curiosity took over as she ran her hand across the bottom, feeling for the edge of whatever was off. And then—*click*. The panel shifted beneath her fingers, revealing a small hidden compartment underneath. Her breath caught in her throat. She'd had this desk for years and never noticed anything unusual.

Inside the compartment, nestled in the dust, was a small, leather-bound journal. The edges were frayed, and the once-smooth leather was now cracked with age. Her hands trembled as she pulled it out and flipped it open. The pages were yellowed, the handwriting delicate and old-fashioned. On a loose piece of paper stuffed inside the cover, there was a message written in faded black ink.

"*Dearest Evie, Keep this safe. What was taken must remain hidden, for the truth is far more dangerous than you know. Trust no one but those closest to you. - A.*"

Cat's heart raced. *Evie—that's my grandmother.* But the message wasn't written in her handwriting. Whoever "A" was, they had trusted her grandmother to protect something—*something dangerous.*

She flipped through a few more pages, but much of the writing was hard to read, filled with references to things she didn't understand. The only thing she knew for sure was that this journal was important. It was a piece of the puzzle. A key to whatever her grandmother had been hiding for so long.

Her mind raced back to the conversation she had overheard earlier. *Stolen...* Could they have been talking about this? About the necklace? And if it really was stolen, how did her family come to possess it? Why was her grandmother keeping it secret?

Cat closed the journal with a soft thud and hugged it tightly to her chest, feeling the worn leather against her skin. A new sense of determination swelled inside her, filling her with a mixture of excitement and trepidation. The weight of the secrets contained within those pages seemed to press against her heart, urging her forward. She needed to know the truth—about the necklace that had been hidden away for so long, about her grandmother's mysterious past, and about the identity of the person who had penned these cryptic entries. The questions swirled in her mind like a whirlwind, each one leading to another. Cat took a deep breath, her resolve strengthening with each passing moment. She wasn't going to stop until she uncovered it all, no matter where the trail might lead or what dangers she might face along the way. The truth was out there, waiting to be discovered, and she was determined to be the one to bring it to light.

Chapter Two

It was late evening in Evelyn's old family home. The warm glow of the setting sun cast a soft light through the windows, painting the hallways in shades of amber and gold. Cat had made her way downstairs and stood on the threshold of the living room, clutching the journal she found in her desk behind her back. Her grandmother, Evelyn, sat in an old armchair, knitting quietly, seemingly lost in thought. Cat hesitated for a moment and leaned into the door frame.

"Grandma, can I ask you something?"

Evelyn looked up, her knitting needles pausing mid-stitch. She smiled warmly, but there was a flicker of something—nervousness, maybe?—behind her eyes.

"Of course, dear. What's on your mind?"

Cat took a deep breath and stepped into the room, feeling the weight of the journal in her hands secured behind her back. She sat down across from her grandmother, searching her face for any sign of discomfort before speaking.

"It's about the necklace. The one you've never mentioned before," she says, trying not to sound too direct.

Evelyn's smile faltered, just for a second, before she looked back down at her knitting, her fingers moving faster now. The clinking of the needles filled the silence between them.

"Oh, the necklace. What about it, sweetheart?" she asks, sounding a little too casual.

"I was on my way to make tea earlier and I overheard you talking about it to a man. He said something about it being stolen... is that true?"

The clinking of the needles stopped altogether. Evelyn's hands were still resting in her lap. For a moment, it seemed like she wasn't going to answer. Cat could sense the tension in the air, thick and heavy.

"Cat, there are some things in life that are better left in the past. That necklace... it's one of those things," Evelyn said in a careful, quieter voice now.

Cat, seeming unsatisfied with the answer, leaned back in her seat.

"But why? I don't understand. If it's just a necklace, why does it feel like there's so much more to it? You've always been proud of all the family heirlooms, but you've never mentioned the necklace before. Why?"

Evelyn looked up, meeting Cat's gaze, her eyes filled with something Cat couldn't quite place—fear, perhaps, or maybe guilt. She sighed softly, putting her knitting completely aside to the small end table next to her chair.

"Cat, there are things in our family's past that I never wanted you to worry about. The necklace... it's tied to some of those things. That's all you need to know."

Cat, now visibly frustrated, slightly raised her voice.

"But you're not telling me anything! I'm not a little kid anymore, Grandma. If there's something I need to know, you have to trust me. Is it really stolen?"

Evelyn's face tightened, and for a moment, she looked much older, as though the weight of years has suddenly settled onto her shoulders. She stood up slowly, turning her back to Cat as she moved slowly to the window and absently gazed out at the trees beyond. The golden light washing over her, but she seemed lost in the shadow. After a long pause, her voice barely above a whisper, she finally spoke in a remorseful tone.

"It wasn't meant to be ours. But it became part of our family, and I've tried to keep it safe ever since. That's all I can tell you."

"Why can't you just tell me the truth about the whole story?" Cat says, standing in noticeable frustration.

Evelyn turned around, her expression soft but resolute.

"Because sometimes, the truth is more dangerous than the lie. And I won't let you get caught up in something you're not ready for. Not yet."

Cat opened her mouth to argue, but Evelyn's gaze was unyielding, filled with a protective tenderness that made it clear the conversation was over. Whatever her grandmother was hiding, she wasn't ready to share it. Not yet.

But this was something that Cat wasn't going to let go.

Cat returned to her room, more frustrated than upset. She had been so close to hearing the truth from her grandmother and getting her questions answered, only to have it slip through her fingers with a stern reply. She flopped onto her bed with the journal still clutched in her hand, the soft thud of the mattress a stark contrast to the turmoil brewing in her mind. Her eyes scanned the room, as if searching for answers on the walls, but her thoughts kept drifting back to the worn leather journal.

She began to thumb through its yellowed pages, searching for any other clues that might reveal the identity of the unknown "A". Perhaps another entry could shed some light on what relation this person was to her grandmother. The questions swirled in her head, making her normal thoughts cloudy, pulling her in with its relentlessness. Was this the same man she had heard in the library earlier in the day? Or was "A" someone from her grandmother's past, an old lover or a family member whose name had been lost to the passage of time? She pushed her brain to think through all the memories she had heard of extended family, scouring her mind for any mention of someone who might fit the reference in the journal. But nothing was clicking, no connections were being made, and the more she thought about it, the more her frustration grew.

She carefully read page after page. The cursive handwriting was difficult to read. Reading and writing cursive was something the schools didn't teach anymore. Evelyn had taken it upon herself to teach Cat the basics. For Evelyn, it was something that she deemed as a failure of the modern school system. Most were normal journal entries, happenings of the day, or thoughts put on paper. She flipped another page, her eyes tired but her mind racing. The quiet hum of the house air conditioning was comforting, but she still felt on edge. She knew she was onto something - she just didn't know what. The journal's entries seemed like normal reflections at first, but now, with each turn of the page, more cryptic messages began to appear, written in the margins and scrawled between the lines.

She stopped at a page near the back, her breath catching as she saw the drawing of the serpent coiled around the necklace. Beneath it were these words:

"The rose guards what others seek."

What does that mean? The drawing of the necklace didn't match the one she had found in the attic, but it was awfully similar. Cat frowned, tracing the drawing with her index finger. Her grandmother had never mentioned the necklace, but this made it seem like it was an important family item if it was one.

The drawing made Cat uneasy. The symbol didn't look familiar, but the sketch of a serpent around a jewel seemed significant. Cat wondered if the necklace she saw in the attic had more meaning than just its appearance of a necklace - perhaps it's connected to a secret society or ancient legend.

She continued to flip the through the remaining pages in the journal. Cat noticed one page that is different from the others. There was a long entry, but it had been scribbled out. She could just make out a date under the mess of ink:

"June 12, 1963 - Something happened"

The date jumped out at Cat, even though she wasn't sure why at first. Her grandmother had mentioned taking possession of the family heirlooms in the 1960s. Could this be the date the necklace came into the family - or traded for something? Cat didn't know what the term "something happened" means, but it gave her a chill down her spin.

Realizing this could be a vital clue, Cat reached for her worn backpack at the edge of the bed and pulled out her trusty sketching notebook, its pages already filled with various drawings and notes. She needed to start keeping track of these mysterious details somewhere other than the journal so she could piece them together properly, or at the very least, brainstorm their potential meanings without fear of discovery. Since the tense discussion with her grandmother was definitively over and clearly not open for further conversation, she began to realize with growing concern that if her grandmother ever caught sight of the journal, it would more than likely be confiscated immediately. That would certainly hinder any further investigation into the mystery of the necklace and effectively close the door on all her burning questions - questions that seemed to multiply with each new piece of information she uncovered.

She quickly started copying the information into her sketch book before having a brilliant thought. She reached into her back pocket and retrieved her iPhone.

She carefully took pictures of every page, ensuring the framing was perfect so all sides of the journal could be seen clearly.

As she reached to the final pages of the journal, she noticed a page that was half torn out, followed by several pages missing fully. It was like someone punched her right in the stomach. She had a gut feeling that those missing pages were critical to the truth.

On the torn piece of paper, there was a fragmented sentence as the rest of the page was ripped out:

"...beneath the rose in the..."

The fragmented nature of the message left Cat with more questions than answers. What does *"beneath the rose"* mean? She racked her brain trying to connect this to something—perhaps a painting, an old piece of furniture, or another family heirloom. Her grandmother always loved roses, and there were rose motifs all over the house.

Her thoughts began whirling through all the locations she had observed roses throughout her grandmother's house and the broader estate. Her grandmother had resided there since her early twenties. The possibilities seemed endless if an item was concealed somewhere on the property. Cat's mind refused to release the urge to search. She felt she had to at least conduct a brief search of some of the more noticeable areas.

Chapter Three

Hawthorn Manor loomed over its estate like a sentinel of time, its dark, red brickwork glistening in the afternoon sun. Constructed in the late 1800s, it had served as both a family home and a monument to the ambitions of Evelyn's late husband James Grant's great-grandfather Charles Grant. A wealthy industrialist and art collector from Boston, Charles sought solace from the hustle and bustle of city life, envisioning a sanctuary nestled in the countryside where his family could thrive amid nature's beauty. He dreamt of a place where the Grants could escape the noise and chaos, finding peace and inspiration in the rolling hills and dense woods that surrounded the manor.

The architectural style was unmistakably Victorian Gothic, with pointed arches and steep gables that drew the eye upwards. Multiple roof lines punctuated the skyline, each one holding its own stories of laughter, sorrow, and the passage of time. As one approached the manor via a wide stone path lined with blooming rose bushes, it became evident that every detail had been carefully considered. Intricate wood carvings adorned the grand porch, a warm welcoming to guests while simultaneously hinting of elegance and wealth. The heavy oak front doors were engraved with floral designs, a testament to the craftsmanship of a bygone era.

Inside, the foyer opened up to reveal soaring ceilings draped in shadows cast by an ornate crystal chandelier. The scent of polished mahogany filled the air; every inch of wood paneling spoke of generations who had walked these halls, their stories etched into the very grain of the wood. Black-and-white marble tiles covered the floor—worn smooth by countless footsteps—and each step echoed with history, whispering tales of the past that seemed to linger in the air.

James' great-grandfather had intended for Hawthorn Manor to be more than just a residence; it was to be a place where art flourished alongside familial bonds. The expansive drawing room showcased portraits of ancestors gazing down upon gatherings filled with laughter and discourse on art, literature, and politics. An eclectic mix of antique furniture whispered tales of lavish parties held beneath candlelight while capturing fleeting moments that would eventually fade into memory. The room was a testament to the family's love for culture and their commitment to preserving it for future generations.

The library remained one of the most revered spaces in Hawthorn Manor. Towering bookshelves held volumes from classic literature to obscure historical texts—all meticulously cataloged by her husband James over the years. It was here that his love for history blossomed under his father's watchful eye, also an art collector and historian. As he thumbed through old journals or pored over books on art restoration techniques, he felt deeply connected to those who had come before him, their knowledge and experiences guiding his own journey.

James and Evelyn had two children. Their son had chosen not to pursue the art world. Real estate investments and banking seemed to be the new frontier. The daughter had chosen to live aboard and concentrate on fashion. Times were changing. The world incapable of the old ways, technology always in the forefront. It saddened James and Evelyn that the arts and culture they grew up in was seemingly being forgotten.

Beyond these well-tended spaces lay rooms often overlooked—dusty corners holding forgotten relics from days gone by. The attic held trunks filled with clothes that no longer fit their owners or toys once cherished, but long since abandoned. The attic was a treasure trove of relics and the like. It was a garage sell buyer's dream.

A small but dedicated staff worked full time at the manor, their daily routines woven into the fabric of life at Hawthorn Manor. They divided their time between cooking hearty meals in the industrial style kitchen, cleaning the endless rooms and corridors, and tending to the manicured gardens that surrounded the estate. Only a select few lived permanently on the grounds, occupying the modest but comfortable quarters in the manor's east wing, while others made the daily journey from the nearby town to perform their duties with quiet efficiency.

Hawthorn Manor's gardens expanded outward like an artist's canvas—a riot of color during springtime when roses bloomed in abundance. They provided a serene backdrop for contemplative afternoons spent wandering through towering hedges and fragrant blooms. For generations, the family tended these gardens not merely as an aesthetic choice but as part of their heritage—a way to connect with nature while preserving memories linked to every flower. Each path and planting was a testament to the family's love for the land and their dedication to maintaining its beauty.

In time, as Evelyn took on stewardship over Hawthorn Manor after her husband James passed away, she felt compelled to preserve both physical objects and stories handed down through generations—each artifact telling pieces of a larger narrative woven throughout history itself. Evelyn made careful choices regarding what art would grace the walls—not just paintings acquired for aesthetic pleasure but those embedded with significance, reflective of personal stories shared between artists and collectors alike over centuries past.

But beneath this surface beauty lay darker truths lurking within shadows cast by memories best left untouched—the whispered legacies from James Grant's time spent serving in WWII became entwined within tales told at fireside chats during chilly evenings spent reminiscing about loved ones lost far too soon—or victories won against overwhelming odds faced abroad, all tied together seamlessly under one roof: Hawthorn Manor, a complex narrative stitched into being through hardships weathered over generations, as the family united against seemingly impossible obstacles looming on their horizon. Each room, each artifact, and each story held within the manor's walls was a testament to the Grant family's enduring spirit and their unwavering commitment to preserving their legacy.

Chapter Four

Cat awoke the following morning with a new sense of purpose, her muscles still tense from tossing and turning all night. She hadn't slept well due to not being able to quiet her mind, her thoughts racing with possibilities and unanswered questions. The early morning sunlight filtering through her bedroom window did little to dispel the fog of exhaustion, but the determination burning in her chest was enough to push her forward. Her grandmother's cryptic behavior and the mysterious circumstances surrounding the necklace kept replaying in her mind like a skipping record. However, the lack of sleep didn't dampen her energy or enthusiasm for searching for more clues around the manor. She pushed aside the lingering doubts about her grandmother's words as she quickly dressed, pulling on her favorite pair of worn jeans and a comfortable sleeveless top, and headed down to the kitchen, looking for something to eat. She didn't want to waste precious time, but she knew she could use the food energy and the opportunity to think through her next move carefully. Where to search first? The question nagged at her as she descended the grand staircase.

Sitting at the large kitchen table, its polished surface gleaming in the morning light, she sipped her steaming tea and methodically thought through the process of the next step in her quest. The warmth of the mug in her hands was comforting as she considered her options. Soon, however, she found herself overwhelmed by the prospect of having so many places to search in the oversized manor. She started to feel like all the questions and lack of concrete information was clouding her judgment, making it difficult to focus on a single starting point. If she was going to find anything of significance, she realized she was going to need a second set of eyes and a fresh perspective.

She finished her tea, the last sip having gone cold, and went directly back to her room, her footsteps echoing in the empty hallways. Her grandmother had been up earlier in the morning and had left for the city to attend an event at the University, as was often the case. The family was always donating or otherwise sponsoring city events, their name a fixture in local philanthropy. Cat quickly fetched her phone from atop her cluttered desk, pushing aside a few sketches and notes she'd made the night before, and fired off a text to her best friend Maya. She knew that if anyone could help her make sense of this mystery, it would be Maya's quick wit and unwavering support.

Cat's fingers flew over her phone's screen as she typed out a message to Maya. "Need your help. Big mystery. Can you come over ASAP?" She hit send and waited, knowing her best friend wouldn't leave her hanging.

Within minutes, her phone buzzed with Maya's reply. "On my way. You got snacks?"

Cat grinned. "Always."

Half an hour later, Maya's familiar knock echoed through the house. Cat bounded down the stairs as a member of the house staff opened the door. Maya stepped through the threshold, revealing a beaming face.

"Alright, Sherlock," Maya said, stepping further inside. "What's this big mystery you've got?"

Cat grabbed Maya's arm, pulling her toward the kitchen. "You're not going to believe this. But first, snacks."

They raided the pantry, emerging with an assortment of chips and cookies. The staff always did a good job of keeping the pantry full of things teenagers would eat when Cat was there for the summers. As they munched, Cat filled Maya in on everything she'd discovered about the necklace and the journal.

Maya's eyes widened. "Holy crap, Cat. This is like, straight out of a movie or something."

"I know, right?" Cat leaned in, lowering her voice. "And get this - I think it might be stolen."

Maya whistled low. "Dang. Your grandma's got some secrets."

Cat nodded, grateful for Maya's presence. Where Cat was cautious and analytical, Maya was bold and impulsive. They balanced each other perfectly, and Cat knew she could count on Maya to push her when she needed it.

"So, what's the plan?" Maya asked, a mischievous glint in her eye.

"We search the estate," Cat replied. "There was something in the journal about 'beneath the rose.' I think it might be a clue."

Maya rubbed her hands together. "Oh, this is gonna be good. Let's go, partner."

As they headed out to explore the grounds, Cat felt a surge of affection for her friend. Maya had always been there for her, through thick and thin. She never judged Cat for her obsession with puzzles and mysteries, instead encouraging her to follow her instincts.

"Hey," Maya said, nudging Cat's shoulder. "Whatever we find, we're in this together, okay?"

Cat smiled, feeling a weight lift off her shoulders. "Thanks, Maya. I don't know what I'd do without you."

"Probably get into way less trouble," Maya quipped, winking.

They laughed, the sound echoing across the estate grounds as they set off on their adventure, united in their quest for answers.

As Cat and Maya ventured into the expansive gardens of Hawthorn Manor, the contrast between the two friends became apparent. Maya's vibrant energy seemed to light up the surrounding space, her dark curls bouncing with each step, and her laughter echoing through the garden. She wore a bright yellow sundress that matched her sunny disposition, a stark contrast to Cat's more subdued attire of jeans and a simple blue top.

Maya had been Cat's best friend since they were kids, drawn together by their shared love of adventure and penchant for getting into mischief, only to cease during the school year when Cat was back with her parents. Her father, chasing investments, moved south to take advantage of not only opportunity but also the tax breaks. But distance couldn't separate their friendship. Where Cat was reserved and thoughtful, Maya was outgoing and impulsive, always the first to suggest a new escapade or challenge. She had a way of pushing Cat out of her comfort zone, encouraging her to take risks and embrace the unknown. Their dynamic was one of balance—Cat's cautious planning complemented Maya's spontaneous daring.

Their friendship had weathered many storms over the years, from schoolyard squabbles to family dramas. Maya had been there for Cat through thick and thin, offering a shoulder to cry on during tough times and a partner in crime for their more daring adventures. They had navigated the complexities of growing up together, and their bond had only grown stronger with each passing year.

As they walked, Maya's eyes darted around the garden, taking in every detail. She had a knack for noticing things others might miss, a skill that had come in handy during their many childhood adventures. Cat knew that Maya's keen eye and quick wit would be invaluable in unraveling the mystery of the necklace. Maya had a way of seeing patterns and connections that others overlooked, making her an essential ally in their quest for the truth.

"You know," Maya said, pausing to examine a particularly vibrant rose bush, its petals a deep crimson against the lush green foliage, "I always knew your family had secrets, but this is next level. I mean, hidden jewelry, mysterious journals—it's like we're in one of those old detective novels your mom used to read to us."

Cat appreciated Maya's ability to find humor in even the most serious situations. It was one of the things that made her such a great friend and confidante.

As they combed through the outer grounds of Hawthorn Manor, their eyes scanning every nook and cranny for anything that seemed out of place. The sun beat down on them, doing its best to dry out the manicured lawns and intricate flower beds.

"Maybe we're looking in the wrong place," Maya suggested, wiping sweat from her brow. "This garden is huge. We could be here all day and still miss something."

Cat nodded, her gaze sweeping over the stone pathways and ornate fountains. "You're right. We need to be more deliberate about this."

They split up, each taking a different section of the grounds. Cat focused on the area near the old gazebo, while Maya explored the hedges that lined the property's edge. They searched diligently, looking for any sign of disturbance or hidden compartments.

After an hour of fruitless searching, the mid-day sun had risen high in the sky, its heat becoming increasingly oppressive. Cat's shirt clung to her back, and she could see Maya's face flushed with exertion.

"I hate to say it, but I think we're striking out here," Maya called from across the lawn. She jogged over to where Cat stood, shaking her head in frustration.

Cat sighed, running a hand through her hair. "I was so sure we'd find something. The clue seemed to point to the gardens."

Maya put a comforting hand on Cat's shoulder. "Hey, don't get discouraged. We've only just started. Maybe we need to approach this from a different angle."

Cat nodded, grateful for her friend's optimism. "You're right. And it's getting too hot out here, anyway. What do you say we head back to the library? We can cool off and maybe find some more clues in the books."

"Sounds like a plan," Maya agreed, already turning towards the house. "Plus, I'm dying for a cold drink."

As they made their way back to the manor, Cat couldn't shake the feeling that they were missing something important. But the coolness of the library beckoned, promising a relief from the heat and perhaps new insights into the mystery that consumed her thoughts.

Cat and Maya entered the library, grateful for the cool air that greeted them as they stepped inside. The room's low lighting and musty scent of old books provided a welcome contrast to the sweltering heat outside.

Cat sank into a long leather sofa, her muscles aching from their fruitless search. She watched as Maya wandered over to a small side table where a pitcher of ice-cold lemonade place by the staff awaited.

"Want some?" Maya asked, already pouring two glasses.

"Absolutely!" Cat replied, reaching out for the drink. The first sip was heavenly, the tart sweetness quenching her thirst.

Maya, ever restless, began to explore the library. She ran her fingers along the spines of what seemed like ancient books, tilting her head to read their faded titles.

"Your grandma's got quite the collection here," she mused, moving from shelf to shelf. "Some of these look older than the house itself."

Cat nodded absently, her mind still churning over the mystery of the necklace. She watched as Maya continued her circuit around the room, pausing now and then to pull out a book that caught her interest.

The library at Hawthorn Manor stretched two stories high, with dark wooden shelves reaching toward an ornate coffered ceiling. Leather-bound volumes lined every available space, their spines a rainbow of worn colors from deep burgundy to forest green. The collection expanding across multiple sections, each dedicated to different subjects that had captivated generations of the Grant family.

In the eastern corner, first editions of classic novels sat protected behind glass cases - Dickens, Austen, and Hawthorne among them. The western wall housed historical texts dating back to the 17th century, their pages faded but preserved with careful attention. Medical journals from the 1800s shared space with illustrated botanical guides, their hand-painted plates still vibrant despite their age.

A rolling ladder attached to brass rails provided access to the upper shelves, where rare art folios and oversized architectural drawings resided. Poetry collections from around the world filled an entire alcove, including volumes so rare that museums had previously attempted to acquire them.

"Look at this," Maya whispered, pulling out a massive book with smooth edges. "It's a first printing of Gray's Anatomy." She carefully opened it to reveal detailed anatomical illustrations, each page protected by tissue paper.

The central reading area featured a collection of maps and atlases spread across multiple centuries, some showing versions of the world that no longer existed. Glass display cases protected the most delicate manuscripts - illuminated religious texts, their gold leaf still catching light, and handwritten journals from explorers long forgotten.

"My grandma said the Smithsonian's been trying to get their hands on some of these for years," Cat explained, gesturing to a shelf of Native American historical accounts. "she always refused. She says they belong to the house."

Suddenly, Maya stopped. "Hey, Cat. This one looks out of place."

Cat looked, her interest barely noticeable. "What do you mean?" She responded without looking up.

"It's newer than the others. And it's not lined up right." Maya reached for the book to retrieve it, her fingers wrapping around its spine.

As she pulled, a noticeable click echoed through the quiet room. Both girls froze, exchanging wide-eyed glances.

"Did you hear that?" Cat whispered, setting her glass down and moving to join her friend.

Maya nodded, her hand still on the book. "It sounded like... a latch opening."

Together, they examined the shelf. Cat ran her hand along the bottom of the shelf, feeling for any irregularities. Her fingers caught a slight protrusion, and with a gentle push, a section of the shelf swung inward.

"O-M-G!," Maya breathed.

Behind the false panel, a small compartment revealed itself. Inside lay another leather-bound journal, similar to the one Cat had found earlier, along with a stack of old papers.

Cat's heart raced as she carefully lifted the items from their hiding place. "These must be more family papers," she said, her voice hushed with excitement.

Cat and Maya settled back onto the worn leather couch, the newly discovered journal cradled reverently in Cat's trembling hands. The leather was cracked and worn, its pages faded with age, a testament to the age of the discovery. With utmost care, Cat opened it, and the musty scent of old paper filled the air, transporting them to a bygone era.

"It's my grandfather's," Cat whispered, her eyes widening with a mixture of awe and anticipation as she scanned the first page. "It looks like some kind of record book, filled with his meticulous handwriting."

Maya leaned in closer, her shoulder brushing against Cat's, her curiosity growing. "What kind of records? Anything juicy?"

Cat flipped through the pages, her brow furrowing in concentration as she deciphered the faded ink. "All sorts. Appointments, meeting places, people's names—some familiar, others completely unknown. There are even records of loans to businesses and individuals. It's like a window into his daily life."

"Whoa," Maya breathed, her voice tinged with disbelief. "Your grandpa was into some serious stuff. It's like we've stumbled onto personal records."

As Cat turned another page, a yellowed slip of paper fluttered out. Maya's quick reflexes came into play as she snatched it from the air before it could hit the floor. Her eyes widened as she examined it. "It's... a sellers receipt... for a LOT of money? For art? Your grandfather was quite the collector, huh?"

Cat nodded, her eyes never leaving the journal, drinking in every detail. "There are more like it. Looks like he had quite the collection. I had no idea how much some of this stuff cost."

Suddenly, Cat's finger paused on a particular entry, her nail lightly scraping the paper. Her breath caught in her throat, and her heart began to race. "Maya, look at this. I think we've found something big."

Maya leaned in closer, her eyes following Cat's moving finger. "It's one of the last entries in the journal, *June 12, 1963—Sterling Galleria - midnight*. What about it? Is it important?"

"That's the same date mentioned in my grandmother's journal," Cat said, her voice tight with excitement and a hint of trepidation. "This has to be connected to the necklace somehow. It can't be a coincidence. I think my grandfather died in 1963 as well. In my grandma's journal there was a sketch of a necklace, same in this one," she looked at the ceiling to ponder. "And midnight? That doesn't seem like a normal business hour to be doing business,"

Maya's eyes widened, realization dawning on her face. "No way. What are the odds? This is like something out of a movie!"

Cat closed the journal with a gentle thud, her mind racing with possibilities and theories. "This is it, Maya. This is the connection we've been looking for. Whatever happened with that necklace, it all leads back to the Sterling Galleria on that day. We're one step closer to unraveling this mystery."

Chapter Five

Cat and Maya exchanged a meaningful glance, the weight of their discovery hanging in the air between them.

"We need to find out more about this Sterling Galleria," Cat said, her voice filled with determination. She pulled out her phone, her thumbs flying across the screen.

Maya nodded, already reaching for her own device. "Good call. If it's still around, we might be able to dig up some dirt on it."

The two friends hunched over their phones, the soft glow illuminating their faces in the dimly lit library. The only sound was the occasional tap of fingers on screens and the rustle of pages as Cat referred back to the journal.

After a few minutes of intense searching, Maya let out a low whistle. "Cat, you're not gonna believe this. The Sterling Galleria is still open for business. And get this - it's one of the most prestigious art galleries in America."

Cat's eyebrows shot up. "Seriously? After all this time?" She leaned over to look at Maya's screen, which displayed a sleek website showcasing elegant interiors and priceless artworks.

"Looks like they've got some serious clout in the art world," Maya observed, scrolling through the gallery's impressive list of past exhibitions.

Cat nodded, her mind racing. "This can't be a coincidence. There has to be a connection between the gallery and the necklace."

She returned to her own search, fingers flying across the keyboard as she dug deeper. Suddenly, her eyes widened. "Maya, look at this!"

Maya scooted closer, peering at Cat's screen. An old digitized newspaper article filled the display, its headline bold and eye-catching: "Controversial Art Auction at Sterling Galleria Raises Eyebrows."

"It's from a few years ago." Cat said, her voice barely above a whisper."

Maya's eyes scanned the article, her expression growing more intrigued with each passing second. "It says here that the auction featured several pieces of questionable provenance. Some experts even suggested that a few items might have been stolen or illegally obtained. It sounds to me like the Sterling Galleria does some shady business."

Cat's heart raced as she read the article. The pieces were starting to fall into place, forming a picture that was both exciting and terrifying. "The gallery must be linked to the necklace in some way. Perhaps that's where my grandfather got it from?"

THE AMARA NECKLACE

Cat and Maya exchanged excited glances, their minds racing with possibilities.

"We have to go there," Cat whispered, her eyes gleaming with determination. "Maybe we can find out more about the necklace and what happened in 1963."

Maya nodded enthusiastically. "Definitely. We could pretend to be art students or something. Get a tour, ask some questions..."

The creak of the library door cut their conversation short. Cat's eyes widened in panic as she saw her grandmother, Evie, step into the room. In a flurry of movement, she shoved the journal under a nearby cushion while Maya hastily closed the browser tabs on their phones.

Evie paused, her sharp gaze taking in the scene. "What are you two up to?" she asked, her tone light but laced with suspicion.

Cat's heart raced as she fumbled for words. "Oh, we were just... uh..."

Maya jumped in smoothly. "We're planning a trip to an art gallery for a summer school project, Mrs. Grant. Cat was telling me about some of the amazing pieces in your family's collection, and we thought it would be cool to see some professional exhibits."

Cat nodded quickly, grateful for Maya's quick thinking. "Yeah, exactly. We were thinking of visiting the Sterling Galleria. Have you heard of it, Grandma?"

Evie's expression flickered for a moment, a mix of relief and something else Cat couldn't quite place. "The Sterling Galleria? Yes, I'm familiar with it. It's quite prestigious." She paused, her brow furrowing slightly. "But you two be careful if you go into the city. Art galleries can attract all sorts of high-class riff raff, you know."

Cat's curiosity piqued at her grandmother's warning. Was there more to this than just general caution? She opened her mouth to ask, but Maya spoke first.

"Don't worry, Mrs. Grant. We'll be super careful. We're just going for research, nothing crazy."

Evie nodded, seemingly satisfied with the explanation. "Well, alright then. Just remember what I said. And let me know if you need any help with your project." With a final visual inspection around the room, she turned and left, closing the door behind her.

As the door clicked shut behind Evelyn, Cat and Maya exhaled in unison, their tense shoulders relaxing. They waited a moment, straining to hear Evie's footsteps fade down the hallway before turning to each other.

"That was close," Cat whispered, fishing out the journal from beneath the cushion.

Maya nodded, her eyes wide. "No kidding. Your grandma's got some serious ninja skills. I didn't even hear her coming."

Cat chewed her lower lip, her gaze fixed on the worn leather cover of the journal. "Maya, do you think we should tell her? About what we found?"

Maya leaned back, her brow furrowed in thought. "I don't know, Cat. She seemed pretty spooked when you mentioned the gallery. And remember that conversation you overheard? She clearly doesn't want you involved in... whatever this is."

"But it's my family history," Cat argued, her voice low but intense. "Don't I have a right to know?"

Maya placed a comforting hand on Cat's arm. "Of course you do. But maybe there's a reason she's keeping it secret. What if it's dangerous?"

Cat's eyes lit up with determination. "That's exactly why we need to find out more. If there's danger, shouldn't we at least know about it?"

After a moment of consideration, Maya nodded slowly. "You're right. We should keep digging. At least until we have a better idea of what we're dealing with."

"So, we're agreed?" Cat asked. "We keep this to ourselves for now?"

"Agreed," Maya confirmed. "Now, about that gallery visit..."

Cat pulled out her phone, already tapping away. "Looks like they're open tomorrow. I'll drive."

Maya grinned, her excitement palpable. "Perfect. I'll tell my mom I'm helping you with a summer project. It's not even really a lie."

Cat laughed softly. "Technically, we are doing research."

They spent the next few minutes ironing out the details of their plan, deciding on their cover story and what questions they wanted to ask.

"Remember," Cat said as they prepared to leave the library, "we're just two art students working on a project about historical auctions. Nothing suspicious."

Maya nodded, her expression serious for once. "Got it. Just two normal, totally-not-investigating-a-family-mystery teens."

As they stepped out of the library, Cat felt a mix of excitement and apprehension. Tomorrow, they'd be one step closer to unraveling the mystery of the necklace and her family's past.

Chapter Six

That evening, Cat sat cross-legged on her bed, the two old journals open in front of her. She flipped through pages filled with drawings of several necklaces that were all similar, scribbled notes, and questions that still needed answers. Her fingers traced the outline of one of sketches of a necklace, her mind racing with possibilities.

The sudden buzz of her phone startled her. Cat glanced at the screen, frowning at the 'unknown caller' on her screen. She hesitated, her thumb hovering over the green answer button. After a moment's deliberation, she swiped to accept the call.

"Hello?" Cat's voice came out quieter than she intended.

There was a pause, filled only with a faint static. Then a voice spoke. It was low and distorted, as if run through some kind of voice changer.

"Catalina Grant," the voice said, sending a chill down Cat's spine. "You need to stop."

Cat's breath caught in her throat. "Who is this?"

"That's not important," the voice continued, ignoring her question. "What's important is that you stop digging into things that don't concern you. You don't know what you're dealing with."

Cat's hand tightened around her phone. "What are you talking about?" Noting that, the voice sounded vaguely familiar.

"The necklace, Sterling Galleria. You're treading dangerous waters, Catalina. For your own safety, and the safety of those you care about, stop your searching now."

The line went dead before Cat could respond. She lowered the phone slowly, her heart pounding in her chest. The room suddenly felt colder, and she wrapped her arms around her waist, trying to process what had just happened.

Cat's hands trembled as she set the phone down on her nightstand. Her heart raced, and she found herself pacing the length of her room, her mind reeling from the cryptic call. The stranger's words echoed in her head, each repetition sending a fresh wave of fear through her body.

She paused by the window, pressing her forehead against the cool glass. The familiar sight of Hawthorn Manor's grounds did little to calm her nerves. Cat took a deep breath, trying to steady herself. Despite the fear coursing through her veins, she felt a surge of determination. The call had only confirmed one thing - she was on the right track.

Cat grabbed her phone again, her thumbs moving rapidly across the screen as she typed out a message to Maya.

"Need to talk ASAP."

Maya's reply came almost instantly. "Call me"

Almost immediately, Cat called Maya. She answered the phone before it had a chance to ring. Cat sat on the floor with her back against the bed as she recounted the phone call to Maya, her voice barely above a whisper.

"They told me to stop digging," Cat finished, running a hand through her hair. "But Maya, I can't. This just proves there's something big going on."

Maya's reply was with great concern. "Cat, this is serious. What if they're not bluffing? What if it is real danger?"

"I know, I know," Cat sighed. "But I can't just let this go. There are too many questions. My family's history, my grandmother's reaction... There's something bigger going on here and I want to know the truth."

Maya quickly switched the phone to her other ear. "I get it. Just... wait until tomorrow so we can solve this together, okay? You gotta be careful now."

Cat agreed, grateful for her friend's support. "I will. But I think we need to know more. We need to dig deeper into the necklace's history. I'm hoping the Sterling Galleria can fill in some of the questions."

"Agreed," Maya said. "Where do we start?"

Cat's gaze fell on her sketchbook, filled with notes and drawings. "We start by connecting the dots we already have. And we stay alert. Whoever made that call must be watching us."

The weight of the situation settled over them, the excitement of their investigation now tinged with a sense of real danger. But as Cat talked it over with Maya, she knew she wasn't alone in this. Two heads were better than one.

Chapter Seven

December 10th, 1944

In the waning days of World War II, as Allied forces pushed deeper into Nazi-occupied territories, the true extent of the Third Reich's cultural plunder became increasingly apparent. Priceless artworks, historical artifacts, and irreplaceable treasures had been systematically looted from museums, private collections, and cultural sites across Europe. The scale of the theft was staggering, with countless masterpieces and relics vanishing into the chaos of war.

James Grant sat in a brightly lit office at the Pentagon, his fingers drumming nervously on the arm of his chair. The young art expert had been abruptly pulled from his unit without explanation, and now he waited, unsure of what lay ahead. The air in the room felt thick with anticipation, and Grant couldn't shake the feeling that something momentous was about to unfold.

James pulled out his father's pocket watch, a family heirloom passed down through generations of art collectors. The gold surface reflected the overhead office light, its face marking another hour of waiting.

The door opened and Lieutenant Colonel Harrison stepped in, his uniform crisp despite the late hour.

"Lieutenant Grant." The Colonel gestured to the empty chairs. "Your reputation precedes you, Lieutenant. The Grants - three generations of art collectors, yes?"

James straightened his back. "Four generations, sir. Started with my great-grandfather in Boston."

"Tell me, Lieutenant," Harrison leaned forward, "what do you know of the Raphael that hung in the Czartoryski Museum?"

"'Portrait of a Young Man', 1514." James didn't hesitate. "Oil on panel, stolen by the Nazis in '39 from Kraków. One of Raphael's most accomplished works from his Roman period." At age twenty-four, he'd already cataloged more masterpieces than most curators saw in a lifetime.

Harrison's lips curved into a slight smile. "And its current location?"

"Unknown, sir. Last seen being transported to Dresden in '42. Though there were rumors it ended up in Hitler's private collection."

The Lieutenant Colonel cleared his throat. "Seems like you are the perfect man for this mission. Follow me."

James followed the Lieutenant down the hall to the "old man's" office. Without knocking, Harrison entered the room and held the door for Grant to enter.

"Take a seat," Harrison said sharply.

After a few minutes, the door opened with a creak, and a stern-faced Colonel Blose entered, his posture perfectly straight. He was followed by a lanky man in a well-worn tweed jacket. James recognized him immediately as John Bowers, a renowned antique dealer from back home. Bowers' presence only added to the mystery of the situation.

"Gentlemen," the colonel began, his voice gruff and authoritative, "you're here because your country needs your expertise." He paused, letting the weight of his words sink in, his gaze moving between the two men.

The colonel pulled out a leather folder and spread several photographs across the desk. "These were taken at a warehouse outside Munich last month. We need someone who can spot the genuine articles among the forgeries. Someone who understands the cataloging systems of Europe's major museums."

James studied the black and white images. Even in grainy photographs, he recognized pieces he'd only seen in art history books - Dutch masters, Renaissance sculptures, medieval religious artifacts.

"Your academic background makes you uniquely qualified," Blose said. "Art history, cultural preservation, European history - all essential for this mission."

"The kind of knowledge that comes from growing up in the business," the Harrison added. "Can't teach that in any military training program."

James touched one of the photographs - a marble bust half-wrapped in protective cloth. "This is from the Uffizi Gallery. I saw it in Florence when I was twelve. My father knew the curator."

"Exactly the type of recognition we need." Blose nodded. "Speed will be crucial. As the Reich collapses, they're destroying evidence - including priceless artworks."

The colonel casually flipped a beige folder in front of Grant and Bowers. James opened the folder, scanning the documents inside. Transfer papers, security clearances, mission parameters. His fingers traced the official seals - American and Soviet side by side.

"We are forming a task force with the Soviets," Blose said as he leaned back in his chair. His posture breaking for the first time. Grant and Bowers exchanged glances, surprise and a hint of apprehension evident on their faces. The idea of working with the Soviets, so soon after being allies of convenience, seemed fraught with potential complications.

"With the Soviets, sir?" Grant asked, unable to hide his skepticism. His mind raced with the implications of such a partnership.

The colonel nodded grimly, his expression betraying a mix of resignation and determination. "I know, it's not ideal. But the scale of Nazi looting is unprecedented. We need all hands on deck, even if it means working with our... less than trustworthy allies." The last words were spoken with a hint of distaste.

Bowers leaned forward in his chair, his eyes gleaming with a mixture of interest and professional curiosity. "What exactly will this task force be doing?" he inquired, his voice tinged with excitement despite the gravity of the situation.

"The war will be over very soon. Soon the clean up will begin and the task force should have the freedom to roam wherever the cases lead, gentlemen," the colonel explained as he stood up and started pacing slowly behind his desk. "You'll be tracking down hidden caches, interrogating Nazi officials, following paper trails. The Task Force will be Top Secret. We don't want treasure hunters from all over the world trekking through Germany collecting priceless art works for themselves. It's vital you locate and secure as much of the antiquities as possible. It's crucial to preserving our shared cultural heritage."

Grant felt a complex mix of emotions wash over him - excitement at the prospect of such important work, trepidation about the dangers involved, and a sense of responsibility that weighed heavily on his shoulders. This was a chance to use his knowledge of art for something truly significant, but the risks were far from negligible.

"When do we start?" he asked, his voice steady despite the flutter of nerves in his stomach.

The colonel smiled for the first time, a thin curve of his lips that didn't quite reach his eyes. "Immediately. Pack your bags, gentlemen. You're heading to the front lines to meet your Soviet counterparts." There was a finality to his tone that brooked no argument.

As Grant and Bowers left the office, the gravity of their new assignment settled over them like a heavy cloak, the weight of responsibility pressing down on their shoulders with each rhythmic step. They were about to embark on a mission that would shape the future of the art world - and perhaps their own lives -

in ways they couldn't yet imagine. The corridors of the Pentagon seemed to stretch endlessly before them, a fitting metaphor for the long and uncertain road that lay ahead. Grant's fingers absently traced the leather briefing folder he carried, its contents already seared into his memory, while Bowers maintained a stoic silence that spoke volumes about the magnitude of what they'd just agreed to undertake. The fluorescent lights hummed overhead, casting multiple angles of shadows that made the sterile hallway feel more like a tunnel leading them toward an uncertain fate.

Thirty hours later, the German air hung heavy with tension as Grant and Bowers stepped into the makeshift headquarters of the Allied Art Recovery Task Force. The building, a former Nazi administration office, still bore the scars of recent conflict. Bullet holes pockmarked the walls, and the acrid smell of smoke lingered in the air, a stark reminder of the brutal war that was more than likely coming to an end in the next few weeks.

A tall, broad-shouldered man in a crisp Soviet uniform stood at the head of a long table, his piercing blue eyes scanning a map spread before him. As Grant and Bowers entered, he looked up, his gaze sharp and assessing. The man's presence commanded attention, filling the room with an air of authority and barely concealed power.

"Gentlemen," he said, his English tinged with a thick Russian accent. "Welcome to Germany. I am Major

Nikolai Sterling." His voice was deep and resonant, carrying easily across the room.

Grant felt a chill run down his spine. There was something coldly efficient about the Soviet officer, a sense of ruthless determination that set him on edge. He was obviously a battle-hardened veteran from the eastern conflict, his face bearing the subtle marks of a man who had seen too much death and destruction.

Bowers stepped forward, extending his hand. "John Bowers, sir. This is James Grant." His voice was steady, but Grant could detect a hint of wariness in his colleague's demeanor.

Nikolai shook their hands firmly, his grip like iron. "Good. We have much work to do." His words were clipped and to the point, brooking no argument or delay.

As the Major began outlining their mission, James couldn't help but notice the stark differences between the Allied and Soviet members of the task force. The Americans stood on one side of the room, while the Soviets clustered on the other, mistrust evident in their body language. The tension was palpable, a silent battle of ideologies playing out in the confines of this small, war-torn room.

Major Sterling seemed oblivious to the tension, or perhaps he simply didn't care. He spoke with authority, detailing the suspected locations of Nazi treasure caches and the methods they would use to recover them. His fingers traced paths across the map, each movement precise and calculated.

"We must move quickly," Sterling said, his voice cutting through the murmurs of conversation. "The Nazis were clever at hiding their stolen goods. Every day that passes makes our job more difficult." His eyes narrowed, a hint of frustration coloring his words.

Grant raised his hand, drawing Sterling's steely gaze. "Major, how do we determine the rightful owners of the recovered items?" He tried to keep his voice neutral, but a note of concern crept in despite his best efforts.

A flicker of something - annoyance? amusement? - passed across Sterling's face. "That, Mr. Grant, is a matter for our superiors to decide. Our job is to find and secure the artifacts. Nothing more." The finality in his tone left no room for further discussion.

The answer didn't sit well with Grant, but he held his tongue. He glanced at Bowers, who gave him a subtle shake of the head. Now was not the time for arguments. The tension in the room seemed to ratchet up another notch.

As the Major continued his briefing, Grant couldn't shake the feeling that there was more to the Soviet Major than met the eye. The man's dedication to the mission seemed genuine, but there was an underlying current of... something. Ambition? Secrecy? Whatever it was, Grant knew that working with Nikolai Sterling would be a complex and potentially dangerous endeavor. He made a mental note to keep a close eye on the Major, even as he listened intently to the details of their upcoming mission.

Major Nikolai Sterling paced before the assembled twelve members of the Allied Art Recovery Task Force, his polished boots echoing ominously in the makeshift war room. The air crackled with a palpable sense of anticipation as he gestured emphatically to a large, detailed map of Germany pinned prominently to the wall. The map was a testament to their meticulous planning, covered in a web of notes, lines, and markers.

"Gentlemen, our mission is of utmost importance," Nikolai declared, his commanding voice carrying a weight that silenced even the most restless among them. His piercing gaze swept across the room, meeting the eyes of each man present. "The Nazis plundered Europe's cultural heritage on an unprecedented scale. Paintings, sculptures, religious artifacts - nothing was sacred to them. Priceless pieces of art, family heirlooms from rich Jewish families, not to mention potentially millions in gold and silver. The depth of their greed knows no bounds."

Grant leaned forward in his chair, his eyes fixed intently on the map. Red pins dotted the landscape like drops of blood, each representing a potential cache of stolen treasures. His mind raced with the possibilities and challenges that lay ahead.

Sterling continued, his voice filled with passion and conviction, "These works aren't mere objects, gentlemen. They are the very legacy of civilizations, the shared history of humanity itself. Every piece we recover is a decisive blow against the darkness that threatened to engulf us all. We stand as the guardians of our collective past."

Bowers nodded solemnly, his expression grave and his brow furrowed with concern. "How many artifacts are we talking about, Major?" he asked, his voice barely above a whisper.

"Thousands, maybe millions," Sterling replied, his voice lowering to match the gravity of the situation. "The scale of the theft is... staggering. Museums emptied, private collections seized, entire cultural identities erased. It's a wound on the face of history that we must work tirelessly to heal."

The room fell into a heavy silence as the weight of their monumental task settled upon them. James felt a complex mix of determination and dread coursing through him. The responsibility was immense, almost overwhelming in its scope.

Sterling pointed to a specific region on the map, his finger tracing the contours of the land. "Our intelligence suggests many of the artifacts were given to the Vatican to hide. This delicate matter is being handled through diplomatic processes. However, our sources also indicate a significant cache hidden deep within the Harz Mountains. Ancient relics, priceless paintings, even entire libraries - all waiting to be reclaimed from the shadows of history."

"And returned to their rightful owners," Grant added, his tone firm and unwavering. His eyes met Sterling's, a silent challenge passing between them.

Sterling's gaze flickered to Grant for a moment before he nodded, a hint of tension in his jaw. "Of course. That is the ultimate goal, Mr. Grant. But first, we must find them. The path ahead is fraught with danger and uncertainty."

The Major proceeded to outline their strategy in meticulous detail, his words painting a vivid picture of the challenges they would face. He spoke of booby-trapped hiding spots left by desperate Nazis, false leads designed to mislead them, and the relentless race against time and nature to preserve fragile artifacts that had already endured so much.

"Remember, gentlemen," Sterling concluded, his eyes sweeping across the room one final time, his voice resonating with purpose, "we are not just recovering objects. We are reclaiming history itself, piece by precious piece. The world is watching us, gentlemen. The eyes of nations and generations yet unborn are upon us. Let's not disappoint them. Our success or failure will echo through the annals of time."

The Allied Art Recovery Task Force headquarters buzzed with activity in the predawn darkness. Updated maps covered the walls, marked with inked drawing indicating possible Nazi storage locations. The smell of coffee and cigarette smoke hung thick in the air as enlisted and officers alike shuffled papers and loaded equipment into canvas bags.

James Grant traced his finger along a map of the German countryside. The coordinates matched intelligence reports of art movements from occupied territories. His knuckles whitened as he gripped the edge of the wooden table.

"Those tunnels won't be easy to access." Sterling's deep voice carried across the room. The Soviet major's boots clicked against the floor as he approached. "My country report heavy Nazi presence in the area, even after surrender."

"When have they ever made it easy for us?" Grant rolled up the map and secured it with a rubber band.

"Never." Sterling pulled out a silver cigarette case. "But this time feels different. The intelligence suggests they're protecting something big."

The room filled with a few more personnel - American soldiers checking weapons, Soviet specialists reviewing documents, intelligence officers comparing notes. The twelve men were made up of six Americans and six Soviets. On the American side, they were mostly hardened soldiers from the invasion of France. Grant and Bowen were the exception. On the Soviet side, all six men had fought on the eastern front. No art experience and no cultural expertise. However, it was clear to both Grant and Bowen that Sterling knew his antiquities. Despite their different uniforms, art and cultural history went across borders. Russia had a long history of cultural art, and almost every child growing up in Russia learned of at least the country's rich history.

"Gear up, we move in thirty." Sterling commanded with a strong Russian accent. His voice commanded immediate attention. "Latest reports confirm increased activity near the target site. We need to move fast before they relocate the artifacts."

Grant packed his satchel with a small leather-bound notebook, pencils, and a new U.S. military prototype camera. His expertise in identifying authentic artwork would be crucial once they located the cache. He added a Colt .45 as a final item - in his knowledge, art thieves rarely surrendered peacefully.

"The trucks are ready." Sterling crushed his cigarette under his boot. "My men have secured the route through the checkpoint at Karlshorst."

"Remember, we're dealing with desperate men," Grant addressed the assembled team. "They know the war is lost, but they'll protect these treasures to the bitter end. Stay alert."

The task force moved with practiced efficiency, loading equipment and supplies into a convoy of military trucks. Grant and Bowers climbed into the lead vehicle with Sterling. The Soviet major unfolded a detailed map of their route across his knees.

The convoy rumbled to life in the gray morning light. James watched the bombed-out buildings of Stuttgart slide past the window. The city bore deep scars from the war - collapsed walls, crater-filled streets, civilians picking through rubble.

"Your hands are shaking." Sterling's observation cut through the engine noise.

James flexed his fingers. "Just eager to get started. Intel guys have tracked these pieces for weeks."

"Patience, my friend. The art has waited this long." Sterling pulled out his cigarette case again. "Though I share your urgency. My superiors grow increasingly... interested in certain items."

The convoy wound through checkpoints and ruins, heading west into the German countryside. Grant reviewed his notes on the reported artwork - paintings by Old Masters, religious artifacts, jewels from noble collections. The scale of Nazi looting still staggered him.

Their vehicles passed a collapsed church, its bell tower lying broken across the road. Workers cleared a path through the debris, barely glancing at the military trucks. Such sights had become commonplace.

"Five minutes to the rally point." The driver's voice crackled over the radio.

Sterling checked his watch and weapon one final time. Beside him, Sterling stubbed out his cigarette and straightened his uniform. The morning sun finally broke through the clouds, casting long shadows across the scarred landscape.

The convoy slowed as they approached an abandoned farmhouse serving as their forward operating base. Local resistance fighters had secured the area, confirming recent Nazi transport activity in the region.

James shouldered his pack, feeling the familiar weight of his equipment. Around him, the task force split into predetermined teams, each with specific search zones and objectives. Their meticulous planning was finally in motion.

As the Allied Art Recovery Task Force pressed on into the heart of the Harz Mountains, their progress impeded by the unforgiving terrain and the ever-present threat of hidden perils. Grant, his brow slick with perspiration, carefully scanned the jagged rock formations for any indication of Nazi concealment.

Just as they made it to a clearing in the forest, gunfire erupted from the tree line. Bullets peppered the surrounding rocks, sending chips of stone flying. Grant dove behind a boulder as the sharp crack of rifles split the morning air.

"Contact front!" Sterling's voice cut through the chaos. "Eight hostiles, moving between the trees!"

The task force scattered for cover. Soviet and American uniforms blurred together as training took over. The sound of bolts clicking and magazines being checked filled the brief pause in firing.

"Bowers, on your left!" Grant shouted as a Nazi soldier emerged from behind a fallen tree.

Bowers swung his Thompson submachine gun around and squeezed the trigger. The Nazi dropped, but two more took his place, their MP40s chattering.

Sterling's precise shots rang out from behind a stone outcropping. A Nazi clutched his chest and stumbled backward into the underbrush. The major worked his rifle bolt with mechanical efficiency, each round finding its mark.

"They're trying to flank us!" One of the Soviet specialists called out in heavily accented English.

Grant spotted movement - three Germans attempting to circle around their position. He drew his Colt and fired twice. The first shot went wide, but the second caught a soldier in the shoulder, spinning him to the ground.

The air filled with cordite and the metallic smell of spent brass. Branches snapped as bullets tore through the forest canopy. Someone screamed - Grant couldn't tell which side.

"Push forward!" Sterling ordered. "Don't let them regroup!"

The task force advanced in practiced coordination. Americans provided covering fire while Soviet team members bounded forward. Then they switched, leapfrogging through the trees with deadly precision.

A German stick grenade arced through the air, landing near Grant's position. He kicked it away just before it detonated, the explosion showering dirt and fragments across the battlefield.

"Clear the ridge!" Grant moved up beside Sterling, both men pressing forward behind the trunk of a massive pine. "They're protecting something up there!"

Sterling nodded grimly. "Two left. Behind those rocks."

The remaining Nazis fought with desperate intensity, but they were outmatched. A burst from the Staff Sargent's' Thompson silenced one. The last German raised his hands in surrender, his weapon clattering to the ground.

Sterling approached the captured soldier, speaking rapid German. The man's answers came in short, frightened bursts.

"He says there's an entrance to the storage facility fifty meters ahead," Sterling translated. "Hidden under brush and debris."

Grant surveyed the aftermath. Two task force members were wounded - nothing serious. Four dead Nazis lay scattered across the forest floor, with three more injured but alive.

"Secure the prisoners," Sterling ordered his men. "Grant, Bowers - with me. Let's see what they were protecting."

They found the entrance just where the German soldier had indicated. Fresh tire tracks in the mud suggested recent activity. Grant checked his weapon and nodded to Sterling.

Bowers wrapped a field dressing around a graze on his arm. "They put up quite a fight for some stolen paintings."

"This is more than just art." Sterling's eyes narrowed as he studied the concealed doorway. "They wouldn't risk their lives for simple paintings. Not now."

Grant helped clear away the camouflaging branches. "Only one way to find out what's worth dying for."

The task force regrouped around the entrance, weapons ready. Soviet and American soldiers who, moments ago, had fought as one unit now exchanged wary glances. The temporary alliance held, but the strain showed around the edges.

Sterling posted guards to watch the prisoners and secure their perimeter. The rest of the team prepared to enter the bunker, checking flashlights and reloading weapons.

The firefight had lasted less than ten minutes, but it changed the atmosphere of their mission. This wasn't just a recovery operation anymore. Whatever lay behind that door had been worth killing and dying for - even after Germany's inevitable surrender.

Sterling, his face a picture of resolve, strode forward. "Tread cautiously, gentlemen. It could be rigged with explosives."

With painstaking precision, they labored to reveal the hidden entrance. As the final boulder was rolled aside, a dark cavern loomed before them. Grant felt his pulse quicken as he stepped inside, his flashlight beam cutting through years of undisturbed darkness.

The beam caught a gleam of gold. Then another. And another.

"My God," Grant whispered, awestruck.

The cavern opened into a vast chamber, brimming with crates, paintings, and artifacts from across Europe. Marble statues stood guard over stacks of ornate books and crates. Jewels twinkled in the flashlight's glow, casting a kaleidoscope of colors on the ancient walls. It was obvious that the placement of the antiquities had been rushed and disorderly.

Sterling's eyes gleamed as he surveyed the treasure trove. "This is only the beginning," he murmured, his voice barely audible. "There must be more."

As the team carefully opened the boxes and crates, meticulously cataloging their find, Grant noticed Sterling's growing unease. The Soviet major paced the chamber, muttering to himself in Russian, his agitation palpable.

"Is something amiss, Major?" Grant inquired, his own suspicion mounting.

Sterling whirled to face him, his eyes ablaze. "This isn't all of it. Our intelligence suggested a much larger cache."

Grant furrowed his brow. "We should be grateful for what we've found. These pieces can be returned to their rightful owners-"

"Returned?" Sterling scoffed, his derision evident. "Do you have any idea of the value of these artifacts hold for the Soviet people? The sacrifices we made as a people?"

The tension in the cavern thickened, the air heavy with unspoken words. Grant stood his ground, his gaze unwavering. "Our mission is to recover and repatriate, Major. Not to argue over spoils."

Sterling's eyes narrowed, his jaw clenched. "You Americans, always so naïve. This isn't just about art. It's about justice. Compensation."

"Gentlemen," Bowers interjected, his voice steady as he stepped between them, attempting to defuse the escalating tension. "Perhaps we should focus on securing what we've found before-"

A flash of brilliant white caught James's eye. Half-buried beneath a pile of papers, an exquisite diamond tiara lay hidden. As he reached for it, Sterling's hand shot out, grasping his wrist with surprising force.

Their eyes locked, a silent battle of wills. In that moment, Grant knew their alliance was built on shifting sands, their shared purpose a fragile truce that could shatter at any moment.

As the tension between Grant and Sterling simmered, threatening to boil over at any moment, Bowers' keen eye caught a sudden flash of brilliant blue amidst the scattered treasures. He knelt down, his hands carefully brushing aside a tattered velvet cloth, revealing an exquisite necklace half fallen out of a beautifully hand carved box that seemed to defy the ravages of time. The piece lay nestled among fragments of broken pottery and tarnished silver, its pristine condition a stark contrast to the surrounding debris. The necklace's chain glinted in the dim light, its intricate work a testament to the skill of a long-forgotten master craftsman.

"Good Lord," he whispered, lifting the piece with reverence, his fingers trembling slightly as they made contact with the cool metal. The weight of history seemed to settle in his palms as he cradled the necklace, its intricate details coming into sharp focus under his scrutiny. Bowers marveled at the delicate balance of the piece, noting how the substantial pendant hung perfectly from the gossamer-thin chain.

Grant and Sterling's heated argument ceased abruptly as they turned to see what Bowers had uncovered. The necklace seemed to pulse with an inner light, its sapphire centerpiece captivating all who gazed upon it. The air in the room grew thick with anticipation, as if the very atmosphere recognized the significance of the moment. Dust motes danced in the dim light, swirling around the men as they stood transfixed by the unexpected discovery. The tension that had been building between Grant and Sterling had dissipated, replaced by a shared sense of wonder and disbelief.

"The Amara Necklace," Sterling breathed, his eyes widening with recognition and a hint of hunger. "I thought it was just a legend, a fairy tale told to aspiring treasure hunters." His voice held a mixture of awe and disbelief, as if he couldn't quite trust his own senses in the face of such an extraordinary find. Sterling's hands twitched at his sides, betraying his desire to reach out and claim the necklace for himself.

Grant stepped closer, his expert gaze studying the intricate lacework and the flawless gemstones. The craftsmanship was beyond anything he had encountered in his years as an art collector. "The Amara Necklace, it's even more beautiful than the stories suggest," he murmured, unable to tear his eyes away from the mesmerizing blue depths of the sapphire. His mind raced with the implications of their discovery, knowing that this moment would forever change the course of their lives and possibly history itself. Grant's thoughts drifted to the countless hours he had spent reading about the Amara Necklace, poring over ancient texts and hearing whispered rumors among curators, never truly believing he would one day stand in its presence.

The history of the Amara Necklace was shrouded in mystery and intrigue, its origins tracing back centuries to the opulent royal courts of Europe. Tales of its beauty and power had been whispered through generations, captivating the imaginations of nobles and commoners alike. The necklace was said to hold secrets that could change the course of history, and its allure was irresistible to those who sought wealth, knowledge, or influence.

The necklace was commissioned in the late 18th century by a wealthy European prince as a gift for his beloved bride, Princess Amara. The prince, utterly captivated by his wife's ethereal beauty and regal grace, spared no expense in the necklace's creation. He enlisted the skills of a renowned master jeweler, whose reputation for exquisite craftsmanship had spread throughout the continent. This artisan, known for his meticulous attention to detail and unparalleled skill, labored tirelessly, pouring his heart and soul into crafting the piece using only the finest materials - solid gold of the purest quality, rare sapphires of the deepest blue, and sparkling diamonds that seemed to capture starlight itself. The jeweler worked in secret, ensuring that every aspect of the necklace was perfect before presenting it to the prince.

The result was a stunning work of art, the Amara Necklace standing as an enduring symbol of the prince's deep and abiding affection. Princess Amara cherished the necklace above all her possessions, wearing it with pride during important ceremonies and lavish social events, where it drew admiring glances and hushed whispers from all who laid eyes upon it. The necklace seemed to glow with an otherworldly light when adorning the princess's neck, enhancing her natural beauty and lending her an air of mystery. It quickly became a symbol of their union and the power of their love, captivating the imaginations of all who beheld it.

However, the necklace's fortunes took a dark and unexpected turn during a period of political upheaval in the early 19th century. The once-stable royal court was plunged into chaos, and amidst the turmoil, the precious Amara Necklace vanished without a trace. Rumors swirled through the palace halls and beyond, each more outlandish than the last. Some claimed the necklace had been stolen from the royal family's collection, spirited away by a disgruntled courtier seeking revenge. Others whispered that a member of the royal family itself had secreted it away, hoping to preserve their legacy in the face of imminent downfall. The disappearance of the Amara Necklace became the subject of much speculation and intrigue, with some believing it had been cursed by jealous rivals, doomed to bring misfortune to any who dared to possess it. The rumors grew so pervasive that even those who had never seen the necklace felt its influence, fearing its power and the secrets it might hold.

For decades, the necklace's whereabouts remained a tantalizing mystery, its legend growing with each passing year. Treasure hunters and historians alike searched in vain, following false leads and chasing shadows across Europe. They scoured ancient texts, interrogated descendants of the royal court, and even employed the services of psychics and seers, desperate to uncover the truth. Then, like a phantom from the past, it resurfaced briefly in the 20th century. An enigmatic art dealer, known for his collection of rare and often controversial antiques, was rumored to have acquired the necklace and sold it through shadowy channels. But before its authenticity could be verified, the Amara Necklace and its new owner vanished once again, slipping back into the mists of obscurity as suddenly as it had appeared. The art dealer himself refused to speak of the matter, taking his secrets to the grave and leaving behind only rumors, speculation, and obvious sudden wealth that manifested in luxurious properties across Europe and a fleet of custom automobiles. Those who dared to question him about the necklace were met with stony silence or, more troublingly, found themselves quietly but firmly removed from his social circles.

The Amara Necklace's legend continued to grow in the intervening years, with whispers of its supposed mystical powers and the secrets it held captivating the imagination of a new generation. Some believed the sapphire at its center possessed the "eye of truth," an ancient power capable of piercing through lies and revealing the darkest secrets of those who dared to wear it. Others claimed the necklace could grant visions of the future or unlock hidden knowledge from the past. These tales, whether born of truth or fantasy, only served to enhance the necklace's allure, drawing in those who sought to use its power for their own purposes.

This aura of mystery and danger surrounding the necklace had made it a coveted prize, sought after by those who craved power and influence in equal measure. Wealthy collectors, occult enthusiasts, and even governments had launched discreet searches for the Amara Necklace over the years, each hoping to harness its rumored powers for their own ends. Some were willing to go to great lengths, employing spies, thieves, and even assassins in their quest to possess the necklace. Private investigators had been hired to track its movements across continents, while shadowy organizations devoted entire departments to uncovering its whereabouts. Museums quietly maintained files on its history, though few would publicly acknowledge their interest in obtaining such a piece. And now, after the necklace found its way into the hands of the Nazi's, who had their own dark ambitions for its supposed mystical properties, the stage was set for a new chapter in its storied history.

Sterling held the Amara Necklace up to the flickering light of their lanterns, its sapphire gleaming with an otherworldly radiance that cast dancing shadows on the cavern walls. The team stood in stunned silence, the weight of their discovery settling over them like a heavy cloak, each member acutely aware that they were in the presence of something extraordinary. The air was thick with anticipation and a hint of unease, as if the very atmosphere was charged with the necklace's mysterious history.

"This... this could be the greatest find of the century," Bowers whispered, his eyes never leaving the necklace. The impeccable lacework seemed to shift and sway with the light, hypnotizing him.

Sterling's eyes narrowed, a calculating look crossing his face as he assessed the situation. His mind raced with possibilities, each one more tantalizing than the last. "We keep this quiet," he said, his voice low but firm. "No one outside this team needs to know about this find. Understood?" His gaze swept over the group, daring anyone to challenge his authority.

Grant stepped forward, his brow furrowed in concern. "Now hold on a minute, Major," he said, his voice steady despite the tension. "We have protocols to follow. This needs to be reported. We can't just—"

"I said, we keep this quiet," Sterling snapped, his voice echoing off the cavern walls, amplifying the finality of his order. "That's an order, Grant. Or have you forgotten who's in charge here?" His eyes flashed in the dim light, a silent warning that he would not be defied.

The tension in the air thickened, becoming almost palpable. Grant's jaw clenched, but he held his tongue, knowing that pushing the issue would only make matters worse. He understood the chain of command, but something about this situation gnawed at him, a sense of unease that he couldn't quite shake.

Bowers cleared his throat, breaking the uncomfortable silence that had settled over the group. "So, what's our next move?" he asked, looking from Sterling to Grant, his expression a mix of curiosity and concern.

Sterling turned to face the group, his expression unreadable, a mask of calm control. "We document everything," he said, his voice steady and authoritative. "Secure the necklace, and continue our search. This changes nothing about our mission objectives." Despite his composed demeanor, there was an undercurrent of excitement in his voice, a barely contained eagerness that belied his stoic facade.

But as the team set about their tasks, cataloging and photographing their find, an undercurrent of unease rippled through the group. The discovery of the Amara Necklace had altered the dynamics of their mission in ways they couldn't yet fully comprehend. Each side felt it, a subtle shift in the atmosphere, a sense that they were now part of something far bigger than they had initially realized.

Grant watched Sterling from the corner of his eye, noting the Soviet officer's barely concealed excitement. Something about Sterling's insistence on secrecy didn't sit right with him, a nagging feeling that there was more to this discovery than met the eye. But for now, he had no choice but to play along, to follow orders and hope that the truth would eventually come to light.

As they carefully wrapped the necklace and placed it back into its wooden container, Grant couldn't shake the feeling that they had stumbled upon something that everyone in the art world wanted. The Amara Necklace, with its mysterious past and whispered legends, had the potential to rewrite the art books. Once word got out about it being found, it would be the target of some of the worlds elite, with the resources to secure it by any means necessary. As the team prepared to move out, the weight of that realization was everyone's mind.

Chapter Eight

Once back at the safe-house, the team huddled around a makeshift table in the dim house, poring over documents they'd uncovered alongside the Amara Necklace. Grant squinted at a faded manuscript, his brow furrowed in concentration, the lines on his face deepening as he deciphered the archaic script. The air was thick with the scent of aged parchment and the faint, lingering smell of gunpowder on their clothes from their earlier encounter. The table was filled with Nazi paperwork and drawings taken from the bunker. Each of them sifted through the files on the table, gathering vital information for ledgers, military orders, and nondescript maps.

"Look at this," Bowers said, tapping the yellowed page with a calloused finger. "It mentions a 'set of seven,' with the Amara as the centerpiece. Each piece is said to be a masterwork of craftsmanship, rivaling the necklace itself."

Grant leaned in, adjusting his eyes with a squint, his breath slightly fogging up the lenses that Bowers wore on the tip of his nose. "You're right. It says here that each piece is a clue to the location of... something called 'Die

Schatzhammer.'" His voice was a whisper, as if the very words were too dangerous to utter aloud.

Sterling's eyes gleamed in the lantern light, reflecting the flickering flame like a predator's gaze, his weathered features cast in sharp relief against the shadows. "Die Schatzhammer? The Vault?" He leaned forward, his voice dropping to a hoarse whisper. "I've heard whispers of it. Supposed to be Hitler's private collection. A hidden repository of the Third Reich's most valuable plunder—art, gold, secrets that could change the course of history." His fingers drummed methodically against the wooden table as he spoke, betraying an underlying tension. "According to our interrogations of a few captured Nazi SS officers, the Germans supposedly etched the location of the vault into certain pieces of jewelry and spread them out across Europe. A clever way to hide their greatest treasures in plain sight." He gestured impatiently toward the evidence before them, his expression hardening with barely contained anticipation. "Unpack the necklace and let's have a look, shall we?"

Bowers located the necklace directly and brought it to the makeshift table and laid it down delicately. Sterling carefully lifted the necklace from its case and turned the pendant over. All three men leaning in as close as they could to inspect its undercarriage. Sterling ran his thumb over the back of the clasp and it separated into two halves. Holding the lantern as close as he could, Grant could see some type of engraving.

"24.22.68.12" Sterling breathed, pausing between each number to ensure he saw it correctly.

Grant grabbed his notepad and pencil as soon as Sterling read the first number, writing it down as Sterling spoke the numbers slowly. After Sterling read the last number, they each stared at each other as if waiting for the other to explain what it meant.

"It's a code," Grant said, looking over the numbers he had just written down.

"That means the intelligence is correct. They coded the location of the Schatzhammer in jewelry," Bowers replied.

"If this is true," Grant mused, taking a step backwards, which provided breathing room, "the Amara Necklace we found is just the beginning. We might be on the verge of uncovering something that could rewrite the history books. There's no telling what the Nazis have gathered from the four corners of the globe."

The implications hung heavy in the air, like the thick smoke from a battlefield. What had started as a straightforward recovery mission had suddenly become a high-stakes treasure hunt, with the potential to regain some of the humanity that had been lost at war. Finally something positive to give the world that was still reeling from conflict.

Sterling paced, his boots echoing off the room walls, the sound a stark reminder of the urgency of their situation. "We need to move quickly. Search the inventory for any necklaces we have. Moving forward, we search every necklace for more codes. We will need all the pieces of the puzzle if we are to find the vault. We must move fast. If word gets out about this, every fortune hunter, spy, and double agent in Europe will be on our heels."

"Not to mention the governments we're supposed to be working for," Bowers added quietly, his eyes darting between his comrades, a hint of unease in his voice.

Grant frowned, the lines around his mouth deepening with concern. "We can't keep this from our superiors indefinitely. They have resources, intel that could help us."

"We can, and we will," Sterling snapped, his voice echoing off the room's empty walls. "At least until we've secured the rest of the set. Think of what we could accomplish with resources like that. The power it would give us."

The tension in the room ratcheted up a notch, like the tightening of a wire about to snap. Grant and Bowers exchanged wary glances, sensing the shift in their mission's purpose. The trust that had once been unspoken now seemed fragile, ready to shatter under the weight of their newfound knowledge.

"Where do we start?" Bowers asked, breaking the uneasy silence, his voice barely above a whisper.

Sterling spread out a map on the table, the paper crinkling under his rough hands. "We follow the trail. The necklace is our key, and these documents might hold clues to the locations of the other pieces. We'll need to decipher these codes, follow these paths, and stay one step ahead of anyone who might know what we now know."

As they began to plot their next moves, the camaraderie that had defined their team started to fray at the edges, like a rope worn thin from too much strain. The promise of untold riches and the weight of their secret created an undercurrent of suspicion, a subtle but growing mistrust that threatened to divide them.

Grant caught Sterling eyeing the necklace with an intensity that made him uneasy, a hunger in his gaze that spoke of more than just patriotic duty. Bowers buried himself in the documents, muttering about patterns and codes, his voice a low murmur in the otherwise silent house. The hunt for the complete set had begun, and with it, the potential for both a great discovery and a dangerous rivalry.

Over the next several long months, the Allied Art Recovery Task Force (AARTF) embarked on a whirlwind of operations across Europe. Their efforts bore fruit as they uncovered cache after cache of Nazi-looted treasures. With each discovery, the team grew more adept at deciphering the information and clues left behind, leading them closer to completing the fabled set of seven. The thrill of each find fueled their determination, pushing them to work harder and move with greater purpose.

Grant and Bowen worked tirelessly, their expertise in art history and cryptography proving invaluable. They pored over ancient texts, deciphered coded messages, and followed leads that took them from crumbling castles to hidden underground bunkers. Nikolai Sterling drove the team relentlessly, his ambition growing with each successful recovery. His piercing gaze and sharp commands kept everyone on edge, pushing them to their limits. The tension within the group simmered beneath the surface, barely contained by their shared goal, threatening to boil over at any moment.

As autumn turned to winter, they found the final piece of the set in a forgotten monastery nestled high in the Austrian Alps. The team gathered in a safe-house outside Vienna, laying out seven necklaces on a worn oak table. Each with their own inscription. The room was thick with anticipation and unspoken rivalries.

Grant ran his fingers over the intricate metalwork of a golden chalice, the sixth item in the set. His eyes traced the delicate engravings, marveling at the craftsmanship. "It's almost unbelievable," he murmured, his voice filled with awe and a hint of trepidation. "After all this time, we've actually done it. We've brought them all together. Why would the Nazis inscribe clues to the vault on these necklaces?"

"It's simple." Sterling walked slowly around the table with one hand behind his back, his polished boots clicking against the wooden floor. "At some point, the Germans knew they weren't going to win the war. As they hid all these items, they had to have a way of getting back to the vault. I'm not familiar of how the American's do it, but in my country, no one man knows everything - it's a matter of compartmentalization, you see." He stopped at the head of the table and leaned forward as he placed both hands on the massive table, his weathered fingers spreading across the oak surface. "They choose items that would eventually make it into the open if found. Pieces that were too valuable to destroy, too beautiful to ignore. Then, they could retrieve the items by whatever means possible, and piece together the vault location. Like a puzzle scattered across Europe, waiting to be solved."

Bowers nodded, his eyes darting between the artifacts and Sterling. The weight of their accomplishment hung heavy in the air. "The question is, what now?" he asked, voicing the concern that had been growing in all their minds.

Sterling paced the room, his boots echoing on the wooden floors. His face was a mask of barely contained excitement and ambition. "Now, we find The Vault," he declared, his voice ringing with authority. "With the complete set, we figure out the code, unlock its location and—"

"And what?" Grant interrupted, his voice sharp as a blade. He stood up, facing Sterling directly. "Turn it over to our superiors as we're supposed to? Or did you have something else in mind, Major?" The accusation in his tone was unmistakable.

The room fell silent, the unspoken accusation hanging in the air like a thick fog. Sterling's eyes narrowed, his hand unconsciously moving to rest on the centerpiece of the collection, the Amara Necklace. The tension crackled between the two men, months of suspicion coming to a head.

It was in that moment that Grant made his decision. He had watched Sterling's growing obsession with the treasures they'd recovered, noted the way the Soviet officer's personal ambitions had begun to overshadow their mission. The hunger in Sterling's eyes when he looked at the necklaces was unmistakable. The Amara Necklace, the lynchpin of the entire set, couldn't be left in such dangerous hands. Grant knew what he had to do, even if it meant betraying everything he stood for.

Later that night, as Sterling, Bowers, and the rest of the small team slept, Grant crept silently through the safe-house. The floorboards creaked softly under his feet as he made his way to where Sterling was snoring. His heart pounded in his chest, threatening to give him away with each beat. With trembling hands, he carefully lifted the Amara Necklace from its resting place on a small table next to his cot. The weight of the box in his palm felt like a judgment. He secured it inside his jacket, feeling the cold wood press against his skin, a constant reminder of his betrayal. Taking a deep breath, Grant slipped out into the cold Viennese night, returning just before dawn.

The first rays of dawn crept through the safe-house windows as Nikolai Sterling stirred from his fitful sleep. His hand instinctively reached for the Amara Necklace, which he'd kept close even as he slumbered. When his fingers met only empty air, his eyes snapped open.

Sterling bolted upright, frantically searching the immediate area. The necklace was gone. He tore through his belongings, scattering papers and upending furniture in his desperate search.

"Where is it?" he roared, his voice echoing through the safe-house.

Grant and Bowers burst into the room, alarmed by the commotion.

"What's going on?" Grant demanded, taking in the chaos.

Sterling whirled on them, his face contorted with rage. "The necklace is gone. One of you took it!"

He advanced on Grant, grabbing him by the collar. "Was it you, Grant? Did you decide to play the hero?"

Grant shoved him off. "I didn't take anything, Sterling. Get a hold of yourself."

Sterling's wild eyes darted to Bowers. "Then it must have been you, Bowers! You've always been too quiet, too observant."

Bowers raised his hands, nervously backing away. "Major, I swear I had nothing to do with this."

"Liars!" Sterling bellowed. He drew his pistol, waving it between the two men. "I'll kill whoever took it. Do you understand? The necklace is everything!"

Grant and Bowers exchanged a wary glance, their hands raised.

"Think about what you're doing, Nikolai," Grant said, his voice steady despite the gun pointed at his chest. "We're on the same team. We didn't take your necklace."

"Then where is it?" Sterling demanded, his finger tightening on the trigger.

Sterling's hands trembled with rage as he kept his pistol trained on Grant and Bowers. "Empty your pockets. Now!"

Grant slowly reached into his jacket, turning his pockets inside out with only a few crumpled papers to show. Bowers did the same, his movements deliberate and careful.

"Your bags!" Sterling barked. "Everything."

Sterling walked them to their bags laying next to their sleeping bags. The two men complied, lifting their belongings off the hardwood floor. Sterling's eyes darted between them, searching for any sign of the necklace.

"Dump them out," he growled.

Grant and Bowers exchanged a glance before unlatching their satchels. They upended them, spilling clothes, documents, and personal items across the floor.

Sterling's frustration grew as he found no trace of the Amara Necklace. He kicked at the scattered belongings, his grip on the pistol white-knuckled.

Grant seized the moment. "Nikolai, think about this. If we had taken it, would we still be here?"

Sterling's eyes narrowed. "What are you saying?"

"There are other team members," Grant continued cautiously. "People with access to this safe-house. It could be any of them."

Bowers nodded. "He's right. We're not the only ones who knew about the necklace."

Sterling's gaze darted between them, uncertainty creeping into his expression. The gun lowered slightly.

"This... this is a betrayal," Sterling muttered, his voice hoarse. "The team, the mission... it's all compromised."

Grant took a careful step forward. "Nikolai, we can still-"

"No!" Sterling roared, raising the gun again. "The Task Force is finished. You hear me? Disbanded!"

He backed towards the door, his eyes wild. He knew at this point, the necklace could be anywhere and finding it would be nearly impossible. "It's every man for themself now. Take what you want, but the necklaces... the necklaces are mine."

With that, Sterling bolted from the room. Shouts and commotion erupted throughout the safe-house as other team members reacted to the chaos.

Grant and Bowers shared a brief, tense look before springing into action. They scrambled to gather what artifacts they could, knowing that their former Soviet teammates would start doing the same.

Grant and Bowers moved swiftly through the halls of the safe house, his mind racing with possibilities and contingencies. Grant knew that time was of the essence and he needed to move quickly to secure as much of the artifacts as possible. The weight of responsibility pressed down on him as he realized he needed the team to do things that weren't in a play book. He knew he could rely on them to act without question in this treacherous landscape of shifting loyalties.

He found Staff Sargent Thompson first, a battle hardened sturdy man with a steady gaze that spoke of unwavering resolve. Thompson didn't know anything about art or culture, but he knew how to shoot. Something that came in handy several times over the last few months, unyielding in the face of danger. The Sargent's presence was a comforting constant in the midst of uncertainty.

"What's the plan, sir?" Thompson asked, falling into step beside Grant with the practiced ease of a seasoned soldier.

"We're taking what we can and getting out," Grant replied, his voice low and tense with urgency. "Sterling's lost it. The mission is compromised beyond repair. Have the men start packing things into the empty crates. Carefully but quickly."

Next, they approached Sergeant Miller, a man with sharp eyes that missed nothing and an even sharper tongue. He was leaning up against a doorframe, taking long drags from his cigarette, his brow furrowed in concern as he noticed chaos beginning to erupt.

"Miller, we're leaving," Grant said, his tone brooking no argument. "We need to salvage what we can."

He looked up, his expression unreadable for a moment as he assessed the gravity of the situation. Then he nodded curtly, falling into a loose formation behind

Thompson. "About time, sir. This whole operation has been off the rails for weeks now."

With his team at the ready, Grant led them quickly to the safe-house's outer barn on the other side of the lot, a cavernous space filled with the loot they had obtained the last several months. The musty wooden structure loomed before them, its weathered boards creaking in the cold wind. The two remaining Americans, Johnson and Peters, were already in the barn, casually doing inventory, their clipboards covered in hastily scrawled notes about paintings and artifacts. Grant quickly filled them in on the situation, his words clipped and urgent, and gave them orders to stand guard at the doors, to ensure that Sterling's team didn't make their way over to them. He watched as they took up their positions, rifles held at the ready, their faces grim with the understanding of what was at stake.

The smaller team now worked quickly and quietly, packing artifacts into unmarked crates with the efficiency of those accustomed to operating under pressure. Now and then, Grant would pause, his senses on high alert as he listened for any sign of Sterling or his loyalists. But the safe-house courtyard remained eerily silent. The only sounds were coming from the other side of the safe-house where the other storage room was located. It was obvious to Grant that Sterling and his men were targeting the other store room where they had placed most of the gold and silver. Grant watched his team working diligently to seal the loot in the unmarked crates, each one a small victory in their race against time.

Thompson wiped sweat from his furrowed brow, glancing at the growing stack of crates with a mixture of pride and concern. "How are we getting all this out, sir? It's a small fortune in artifacts."

Grant pulled out a well-worn slip of paper from his breast pocket, a name and number scrawled across it in faded ink. "An old family friend from my father's days in the field. He owes him a favor, and now it's time to collect. Keep working. I'll be back as soon as I can."

He stepped away from the others and commandeered the jeep. He noticed his fingers trembled slightly from the adrenaline coursing through his veins. He made his down the winding mountain road and into town below. They had passed a U.S. Army Medical battalion field unit that had set up shop there a few days before. Grant knew they would have communications equipment to civilization. As he approached the main tent, he slammed the brakes, setting the parking brake as he turned the engine off. The jeep had not even stopped rolling. He stepped into the tent and the sentry snapped to attention. Grant didn't waste any time, asking where the landline was and if it was working. The sentry immediately showed him to the small communications setup and pushed the sitting private aside so Lt. Grant could man the station. Grant nervously picked up the receiver and asked the switchboard operator to patch a call to Paris. The conversation was brief and laden with coded phrases, a dance of words that concealed their true purpose. Grant hung up, his expression grim but determined.

Feeling a little more confident, Grant made his way back to his jeep and up the dirt mountain road to the safe-house above the town, but not before a quick deter to pick something valuable up that he had hidden that early morning. As he pulled into the safe-house courtyard, he could see the Sterling and team loading the unit's truck with boxes he knew contained gold, silver, and other works of art. It was clear to him that the Soviets were after the monetary things, not realizing that the real value was being packed up by his team on the other side of the property.

"We have a truck," he announced to his team, his voice tight with suppressed tension. "It'll be here in an hour. We need to be ready to move at a moment's notice."

Miller nodded, hefting another heavy crate onto the growing stack with a grunt of effort. "We'll be ready, sir. Let's just hope Sterling doesn't come over here with his goons in tow."

Grant wasn't worried about Sterling. He had the six necklaces and now all the gold and silver. Grant checked his watch for what felt like the hundredth time, his jaw set in a hard line of determination. Time was ticking away relentlessly, but they were making good progress despite the odds stacked against them. They just had to hold out a little longer to see this improvised plan through to its conclusion. The fate of countless priceless artifacts—and perhaps their own lives—hung in the balance.

The distant rumble of an engine cut through the tense silence. Grant peered through a gap in the barn doors, his shoulders relaxing at the sight of a canvas-covered military truck rolling into the courtyard. The vehicle bore French military markings - his contact had come through.

"That's our ride." Grant waved his team forward. "Move fast, stay quiet."

Thompson and Miller formed a chain, passing crates from hand to hand while Johnson and Peters remained on lookout. The French driver, a weathered man with sharp eyes, met Grant at the back of the truck, handing him several thick envelopes, then proceeded to help stack the cargo efficiently in the truck bed. No one spoke beyond essential instructions, the loading conducted with practiced precision.

A crash echoed from the other side of the compound. Grant's head snapped toward the sound. Through the gathering dusk, he caught glimpses of Sterling's men still hauling their own cargo, oblivious to the operation happening just a few hundred yards away.

"Sir." Thompson's urgent whisper drew Grant's attention back. "Last crate's loaded."

Grant nodded, mentally counting the precious cargo now secured beneath the canvas. His fingers brushed against the small package in his jacket pocket - insurance, in case things went sideways.

"Mount up," he ordered. "Thompson, you're with me in the lead jeep. Miller, Bowers - ride in the truck. Keep those artifacts safe."

"What about us, sir?" Johnson and Peters were trotting from the door.

"I want you two to hustle down to the Medical Battalion in town. Pass a message to COL Blose that Major Sterling has betrayed the team and is taking the treasure east towards Soviet lines."

The men grabbed their packs and moved out the back door without hesitation. Grant slid behind the wheel of his jeep, Thompson climbing in beside him. The French truck rumbled to life behind them, its headlights cutting through the growing darkness.

Grant eased the jeep forward, leading their small convoy through the compound's gates. His knuckles whitened on the steering wheel as they passed the Soviet vehicles, but Sterling's men remained focused on their own operation.

The road stretched before them, a ribbon of packed dirt winding through the German countryside. Grant kept the speed steady, not wanting to draw attention with excessive haste. In his rearview mirror, the truck followed at a careful distance, its precious cargo hidden beneath military-grade canvas.

Thompson broke the tense silence. "Two hours to the station?"

"If we're lucky." Grant checked his watch. "Roads should be clear at this hour."

They passed abandoned farmhouses and bomb-cratered fields, remnants of a war not long ended. The air carried a bite of cold through the open jeep, but Grant barely noticed, his mind fixed on the journey ahead.

A sudden pop from the truck's engine sent Grant's heart racing. He watched the rearview mirror as the vehicle slowed, black smoke curling from under the hood. The driver managed to ease it onto the shoulder before it died completely.

"Damn it." Grant pulled the jeep over, gravel crunching under the tires.

The French driver already had the hood up, waving away clouds of smoke. Miller and Bowers stood guard while Grant assessed the situation.

"Fuel line's shot," the driver reported in accented English. "I can fix it, but it'll take twenty minutes."

Grant scanned the empty road, acutely aware of their vulnerability. "Make it fifteen."

The repair work proceeded in tense silence, punctuated only by the clink of tools and the driver's occasional muttered French. Grant paced the roadside, checking his watch obsessively, while Thompson maintained a vigilant watch.

True to his word, the French driver had them moving again in fifteen minutes. Grant pushed the pace slightly faster now, making up for lost time. The countryside rolled past in deepening shadows, each mile bringing them closer to their goal.

The moon rose, casting silver light across the landscape. Grant drove mechanically, his thoughts racing ahead to the train station and what awaited them there. The weight of responsibility pressed down on him - not just for the artifacts, but for the men who'd trusted him with this improvised escape.

Lights appeared on the horizon - the outskirts of the town where the train station waited. Grant reduced speed, adopting a casual approach that wouldn't draw attention from the military police patrolling the streets. The truck followed his lead, maintaining its distance as they wound through the quiet streets.

The station loomed ahead, its platforms mostly deserted at this late hour. Grant pulled into the loading area, where a small chain of freight cars and engine sat waiting on a siding track. A figure emerged from the shadows - another contact, right where they were supposed to be.

Grant stood on the platform, his eyes darting between the towering stacks of crates and the steam-belching locomotive that loomed before him. The night air was thick with tension, a palpable weight that settled on his shoulders as his small team worked swiftly and silently to load the precious cargo onto the train bound for the coastal port. Each crate represented a small victory, a piece of history rescued from the chaos that threatened to engulf them all. The weight of their mission pressed down on Grant, reminding him of the high stakes, not to mention the families that deserved their heirlooms back, was all riding on their success.

Thompson approached, wiping grime and sweat from his calloused hands with a rag that had seen better days. "Last of it's loaded, sir. We're ready to move," he reported, his voice low and gruff, tinged with both exhaustion and determination.

Grant nodded, his jaw set in a grim line, then turned his attention to a pair of railway officials who hovered nearby. Their expressions were a mixture of curiosity and suspicion, eyes darting between the crates and the small team of men who guarded them so fiercely. With practiced ease born of years in the shadowy world of high-class art deals, Grant pulled out an envelope thick with cash he had gathered from the loot, pressing it discreetly but firmly into the lead official's hand.

"For your trouble," Grant murmured, his voice low but firm, brooking no argument. "I trust there won't be any issues with our journey?" His piercing gaze locked onto the official's face, conveying the gravity of the situation without words.

The official's eyes widened slightly at the weight of the envelope, then narrowed in understanding as the implications sank in. He pocketed it swiftly, nodding with a newfound eagerness to please. "No issues at all, sir. You'll have a smooth ride to the coast. I'll see to it personally."

As the train lurched into motion with a hiss of steam and the grinding of metal on metal, Grant allowed himself a brief moment of relief. The first step of their perilous journey was underway. But the respite was short-lived as they approached the first checkpoint, a gauntlet of British armed guards and probing questions that loomed ahead like a fortress. He tensed, every nerve on high alert, watching as Miller smoothly handed over their military supply papers to a stern-faced inspector whose eyes seemed to miss nothing.

The inspector's gaze flicked between the documents and their faces, his expression unreadable as stone. Grant was holding his breath without realizing it. He had no alternate plan of action should their carefully crafted ruse fail. The seconds stretched into an eternity, each tick of his watch echoing like thunder in the tense silence.

Finally, after what felt like hours, the inspector nodded, handing back the papers with a grunt. "All seems to be in order. Safe travels," he said, stepping back from the train with a wave to his subordinates.

As the train picked up speed again, wheels clacking rhythmically on the tracks, Grant exhaled slowly, feeling some of the tension drain from his body. He exchanged a look of cautious optimism with Thompson, Bowers and Miller, a silent acknowledgment of the bullet they had just dodged. They had cleared the first hurdle, but the night was far from over. The race to the coast, and the promise of safety it held, had only just begun. Ahead lay miles of uncertain territory, each turn of the wheels bringing them closer to either salvation or disaster.

A few hours later, Grant stood on the bustling docks, his eyes fixed on the massive cargo ship that loomed before him. The sun rising in the east and casting long shadows on the water from the shoreline cranes that towered overhead. The salty sea air whipped at his face as he watched the last of the crates being carefully loaded into the vessel's hold. Each crate represented a small victory, a piece of history rescued from the chaos they had narrowly escaped. The weight of their mission pressed heavily on his shoulders as he observed the loading process with a mixture of relief and apprehension.

Nearby, Thompson, Bowers and Miller blended seamlessly into the crowd of dock workers and sailors, their watchful gazes scanning for any sign of trouble. Grant allowed himself a small hand salute of appreciation for their vigilance before turning his attention to the next crucial step of their journey.

With practiced ease, Grant approached the ship's executive officer, a portly man with a clipboard and a 'couldn't care less' expression. Adopting the demeanor of a weary civilian traveler, Grant produced a set of forged supply shipment manifests and a thick envelope of cash.

"I'd like to book passage, if there's still room available," Grant said, his voice deliberately casual despite the tension thrumming through his body.

The purser's eyes widened slightly at the sight of the cash, then narrowed as he scrutinized the documents. Grant held his breath, every muscle taut as he waited for the man's verdict. After what felt like an eternity, the purser nodded, pocketing the envelope with a swift motion.

"Of course, sir. We have a few berths left," the purser replied, his tone suddenly accommodating. "Follow me, and I'll show you to your quarters."

As Grant followed the purser up the gangplank, he cast one last glance over his shoulder at the docks. Bowers, Thompson, and Miller had already disappeared into the crowd, set to return to the safe-house to secure whatever Sterling and his crew couldn't fit into their truck. Now that the crates were safely stowed, and their escape route was secured, Grant couldn't shake the feeling that their ordeal was far from over. As the ship's horn blasted, signaling its imminent departure, he steeled himself for whatever challenges lay ahead.

Grant stood on the deck of the cargo ship as it approached the small, private dock on the outskirts of a sleepy coastal town. The salty air whipped through his hair, carrying with it the tang of seaweed and distant shore. He watched the shoreline grow closer, his heart pounding with a mixture of relief and apprehension. After weeks at sea, navigating treacherous waters and dodging potential threats, they had finally reached American soil. But Grant knew all too well that the most delicate part of their operation was about to begin.

As the ship eased into the dock with a low groan, its hull scraping against the weathered wooden pylons, Grant's eyes darted around, scanning for any sign of unwanted attention. The dock was mercifully deserted, save for a handful of trusted operatives he had painstakingly arranged to meet through family connections. Under the cover of darkness, with only the faint glow of a crescent moon to illuminate their work, they began the painstaking process of unloading the precious cargo.

Grant supervised the operation with laser focus, his body tense and alert. His hand never strayed far from the concealed weapon at his hip, the cold metal a constant reminder of the danger they faced. Each crate was handled with the utmost care, as if containing priceless Ming vases rather than war spoils. The men transferred the cargo from the ship to waiting trucks with practiced efficiency, their movements fluid and purposeful. They worked in near-silence, the only sounds the soft thud of boots on wood and the occasional creak of a crate being shifted. The men communicated through subtle gestures and nods, a language of secrecy they had perfected over years of either smuggling moonshine or who knows what else. Grant didn't ask questions and didn't want to know.

As the last of the artifacts was secured, wrapped in layers of protective material and nestled in its nondescript crate, Grant approached the lead man. The man was stocky, with a weathered face that spoke of years spent in the harsh elements and steely eyes that missed nothing. He stood at attention as Grant drew near, his posture betraying a military background.

"Everything's set for transport to Hawthorn Manor," the man murmured, his voice barely audible above the lapping waves and the distant cry of a night bird. "We've mapped out a route that should avoid any unnecessary attention. Back roads and little-used highways all the way."

Grant nodded, a wave of relief washing over him. He allowed his shoulders to relax a fraction, though his guard remained up. "Good. Make sure the convoy splits up and takes different roads. We can't risk losing everything if one truck is stopped or followed. I'll make sure the house is empty when you arrive," Grant handing them a neatly folded piece of paper. "Follow these instructions carefully."

The man grunted in agreement, then hesitated. His brow furrowed, and he glanced around before leaning in closer. "Are you sure about this, sir? Hiding all of this at your family estate... It's a big risk. If anyone were to find out—"

"It's the safest place I know," Grant cut him off, his tone requiring no argument. His eyes flashed with a determination that silenced any further protest. "No one will think to look there. It's hiding in plain sight, and we have the resources to keep it secure. Just make sure it's all delivered to the location that's on that piece of paper. No one else needs to know about its existence. I trust you and your men will forget everything being done here tonight."

With a final nod, accepting the finality in Grant's voice, the operative moved off to relay the instructions to his team. Grant watched as the trucks were loaded, each one carefully packed to avoid any telltale sounds or shifting that might betray their precious contents. The vehicles departed at staggered intervals, melting into the night like ghosts, to avoid drawing suspicion from any late-night travelers or patrolling authorities.

As the last truck disappeared into the darkness, its red taillights fading around a distant bend, Grant allowed himself a moment to breathe. He inhaled deeply, filling his lungs with the cool night air, as if trying to expel the tension that had built up over the past weeks. The weight of their precious cargo was finally lifted from his shoulders, at least for now. But as he turned to face the ship that had brought them this far, Grant knew that this was only the beginning. The true test would come in the days and years ahead, as they worked to protect and preserve the priceless artifacts they had rescued from the chaos of war.

Grant knew what he had to do. He couldn't just go home and act like nothing happened. He was on orders and by this point, people would surely be looking for him back in Europe. Although Bowers had a cover story, it wouldn't hold up under much scrutiny. He knew the only thing to do was to smuggle himself back to Europe. The urge to just go home was almost overwhelming. He was only a few hours away. But the consequences of doing such would more than likely mean a dishonorable discharge, and possibly prison for military abandonment. Something that would not only tarnish his reputation, but bring dishonor to his family name. As Grant stood on the docks, he knew he only had one choice. Return to Germany, blame Sterling for the heist, and report everything had been stolen by the Soviets.

The military headquarters in occupied West Berlin loomed against the gray autumn sky, its weathered facade bearing fresh scars from the recent bombing campaigns. James Grant climbed the stone steps, his boots echoing through the empty corridor. His uniform hung loose on his frame after weeks of pursuit across Eastern Europe.

The guard at Colonel Matthews' office checked his credentials and waved him through. The smell of tobacco and coffee permeated the room as Grant entered.

"At ease, Grant." Colonel Matthews didn't look up from his papers, his silver-rimmed glasses reflecting the lamplight. "I trust you have news about the Sterling situation?"

Grant's fingers brushed against the empty leather pouch in his pocket - the one that should have contained the manifest of recovered artworks. "The Soviets played us, sir. They'd been planning it from the start."

Matthews set down his pen and leaned back in his chair. The wood creaked under his weight. "Tell me everything."

"We tracked the convoy to Dresden. Sterling had divided the artwork between two trucks. By the time we caught up, he'd already moved half the collection across the Soviet zone." Grant's jaw clenched. "He knew exactly what he was doing, using our joint task force credentials to move freely across checkpoints." Grant had been thinking about this moment for the last two weeks on the voyage back across the Atlantic. He formulated a story so good it would be almost impossible for his superiors to confirm.

"The gold?"

"Gone. Along with the Vermeer and most of the silver." Grant pulled out a crumpled map and spread it on the colonel's desk. Red marks traced Sterling's escape route. "He had a network of safe houses already set up. Must have been planning this for months." Grant actually had no idea what Sterling was up to or to where he had disappeared.

Colonel Matthews studied the map, his weathered fingers tracing the marked locations. "And the Soviet team?"

"They all dispersed. Can't find any of them." Grant's reply held no humor.

"Politics." Matthews spat the word like a curse. "Washington won't risk confronting Moscow over this. Not with tensions already running high here in Berlin with separating the city. Art is the last thing on anybody's mind." He pulled out a silver case filled with hand made cigarettes and offered one to Grant, who declined.

"Sir, give me another week. I can see if we have missed anything and-"

"No." Matthews struck a match, the flame casting sharp shadows across his face. "You've done enough, Grant. There are greater concerns than art theft now. The Soviets' actions here have... complicated things between our nations."

Grant's fist tightened. "The artifacts we recovered - they belong to the rightful owners, not locked away in some Soviet vault."

"Or perhaps they belong to a museum?" Matthews blew out a stream of smoke. "The war's over, Grant.

Time to let the diplomats earn their pay." He pulled out a folder and slid it across the desk. "Your transfer papers. You're being reassigned stateside where you will be honorably discharged."

"Sir-"

"That's an order, Lieutenant. Your flight leaves tomorrow morning from Tempelhof. The rest of the men have already been reassigned to different units. Bowers has asked for a re-assignment to Italy to work with the Italians on restoring their own art collection." Matthews stood and extended his hand. "You did good work here. The brass - they won't forget what you tried to do."

Grant shook the offered hand, feeling the weight of failure pressing down on his shoulders.

"One more thing, Grant." Matthews' voice stopped him at the door. "Whatever the Soviets are planning with those artifacts... sometimes it's better not to know. Go home. Live your life. We won the war."

Grant nodded stiffly and stepped into the corridor. The guard outside snapped to attention, but Grant barely noticed. His mind was already racing through the details of getting home and figuring out what to do with the treasure now in his own vault. A wave of guilt came over him for not giving it to his superiors, but he knew exactly what they would do with it. It would be locked away in some government vault, or displayed in sterile museum cases instead of being given to its rightful owners. He knew the chances of finding the proper owners of the looted treasures was going to be tough, maybe impossible. If the staggering numbers being reported of how many people were killed in concentration camps were correct - and Grant had seen enough during the war to believe they were - it was likely that the true owners and their entire families would never be found. The Nazis had been thorough in their extermination, leaving precious few survivors to claim what was rightfully theirs. The thought made his stomach turn.

The autumn wind cut through his uniform as he descended the headquarters steps. Berlin sprawled before him, a city divided, its ruins slowly being cleaned up. He wondered about Sterling as he embarked a waiting car. Somewhere in Europe, Nikolai Sterling was putting his plans in motion.

Chapter Nine

As soon as he disbanded the task force, chaos ensued. Major Nikolai Sterling moved with frantic urgency, his military training kicking in despite the illicit nature of his actions. He barked orders in Russian to his men and they quickly secured the location of the gold and silver. They grabbed whatever treasures he could find—crates with bars of gold, ornate vases, gilded frames, and jewel-encrusted trinkets—hastily tossing them into the back of the waiting truck with little regard for their delicate nature.

He knew the Americans were taking control of what they could. Sweat beaded on his furrowed brow as he demanded they worked faster, his breath coming in short, panicked gasps that misted in the cool night air.

Just as they finished loading the last of the loot—a small wooden box that contained six priceless necklaces. His heart pounding like artillery fire in his chest, he slammed the truck's rear doors shut with a resounding clang and scrambled into the driver's seat of the first truck; the springs creaking beneath his weight. With shaking fingers that had once effortlessly maneuvered the controls of countless military vehicles, he fumbled with the key before finally turning it in the ignition.

The engine roared to life with a deafening growl, and Sterling led the trucks out of the compound and to the north. A wave of relief washed over Sterling as he realized he had escaped with gold and silver worth maybe millions, the adrenaline coursing through his veins making his hands shake on the wheel. He pressed down on the accelerator; the truck lurching forward as he put distance between himself and the American-controlled villages to the south. The stolen treasures rattled and clinked in the back, safely concealed from prying eyes but serving as a constant reminder of his betrayal. As the compound faded into the distance, Sterling allowed himself a small, grim smile. He had gotten away with it, but he knew that this day would haunt him for years to come, the Amara Necklace taken from right underneath his nose.

Sterling's heart raced as they sped away from the compound, his mind already calculating his next move with the precision of a military strategist. He knew he couldn't stay in Germany—not with the U.S. Military knowing what happened. He was sure that Grant had immediately reported the demise of the task force and was more than likely trying to figure out their next steps. Going back to the Soviet Union wasn't the best choice either. Sterling knew that everything would be confiscated and he would end up with nothing. As his mind raced, he couldn't shake the feeling that Grant had something to do with the disappearance of the Amara

Necklace. He needed to stay close to him and find out if he truly had it or not. Sterling's mind day dreamed about retrieving the necklace and discovering where the Nazis had put their most valued loot. If he was going to keep track of Grant, the United States was the place to do it. Not only could he keep Grant close, but it was a vast land of opportunity where he could disappear into the crowd and start anew, leaving behind the tangled web of European and Soviet espionage.

As dawn broke, painting the sky in hues of pink and gold, Sterling pulled the trucks into a small, nondescript town, its cobblestone streets still quiet in the early morning hours. He found a rotary phone in the telegram office. With trembling fingers, dialed a number he'd memorized years ago, praying it was still active. After three rings that seemed to stretch into eternity, a gruff voice answered, thick with sleep and suspicion.

"It's me," Sterling said, his voice low and urgent, eyes darting around to ensure he wasn't overheard. "I need passage to the United States. Now."

There was a long pause on the other end, filled with the weight of unspoken questions. "Jesus, Nikolai. What have you done this time?"

"No questions," Sterling snapped, his nerves fraying. "I have a truck load of luggage as well. Can you help me or not?"

Another pause, longer this time, fraught with indecision. "Fine. I'll give you an address. Come alone. And Nikolai? Make sure you're not followed." The caller gave him an address and directions of where to meet.

Sterling hung up and hurried back to his truck, his heart pounding in his ears. He drove to an abandoned warehouse on the outskirts of town, its rusted metal walls a testament to forgotten industry. As he waited in the shadows, he ordered his men to reconfigure the load from two trucks down to one truck. They did as they were ordered. Once completed, he huddled the men as if to thank them. As the men gathered in a tight circle, five gunshots rang out into the night in rapid succession. Sterling stood over the five bodies for a few minutes to ensure the job was done. And now, he was alone as required.

Two hours later, right on schedule, a sleek black sedan pulled up, its engine purring quietly. A man in a crisp charcoal suit stepped out, his face a mask of disapproval and concern.

"You're playing a dangerous game, Nikolai," the man said, his voice barely above a whisper. "The stakes are higher than ever."

Sterling nodded, feeling the weight of his actions pressing down on him. "I know. But I need this, Ivan. One last favor. After this, you'll never hear from me again."

Ivan sighed, a sound filled with resignation and a hint of pity. He reached into his coat and handed Sterling a thick manila envelope. "Passage on a cargo ship leaving Hamburg tonight. I'll clean your file back home. You should be off the books from here. I'll make it as if the task force never existed from our side. After this, we're done. Our debt is settled. Understood?"

Sterling took the envelope, relief washing over him like a cool wave. He clutched it to his chest, feeling as though he were holding his very future in his hands. "Understood. Thank you, your debt is settled."

As Ivan drove away, tires crunching on gravel, Sterling allowed himself a moment to breathe, savoring the crisp morning air. He had his escape route, a lifeline thrown to a drowning man. Now, he just needed to make it to Hamburg without getting caught, navigating the treacherous waters between his past and his uncertain future. With one last look at the rising sun, Sterling climbed back into his truck, ready to embark on the most foreign journey of his life.

Sterling arrived at a northeast port in the United States. His entry papers were barely checked by the officials as he debarked. The United States was having an influx of immigrants due to the war, and now the drawing of the iron curtain through Europe. Hundreds of immigrants were coming from Europe each day. The United States officials at the borders were overwhelmed by applicants and asylum claims.

Sterling hired an Irish owned moving company to transport his shipment to a city north of Grant's hometown, carefully selecting a firm known for its discretion and efficiency in handling delicate cargo. His new identity was firmly in place and his stolen treasures carefully hidden away in a small storage facility on the edge of town, secured behind three heavy locks and a worthy alarm system. The quaint New England town, with its tree-lined streets and historic architecture, seemed a far cry from the war-torn landscapes of Europe he'd left behind. Row after row of pristine colonial homes and well-tended gardens painted a picture of peaceful Americana that felt almost surreal after years spent hunting through bombed-out museums and ransacked bunkers. Children played freely on sidewalks while their mothers chatted on wraparound porches, and elderly couples strolled arm-in-arm through manicured town squares. But Sterling knew appearances could be deceiving, and beneath the town's charming exterior lay the perfect cover for his true intentions. The very normalcy of the place, its air of innocence and propriety, would serve as an ideal smokescreen for the dangerous game he was about to play. Here, among the church socials and garden clubs, who would suspect the presence of a former Soviet major with a cache of Europe's lost treasures?

Within a year, using the funds he'd acquired through his illicit activities during the war and subsequent art dealings, Sterling purchased a stately building in the heart of the town's upscale district. The structure, with its ornate Victorian facade, soaring windows, and spacious interior, was ideal for his purposes - both legitimate and otherwise. Over the next few months, he poured his resources into transforming the space into the Sterling Galleria, a high-end art gallery that would serve as both his public face and his covert base of operations. Skilled craftsmen were brought in to restore the original architectural details, while modern security systems were discreetly installed behind the classical moldings. The basement level, accessible only through a private elevator, was reinforced and climate-controlled - perfect for storing items that would never see the public gallery floors above.

As the gallery took shape, Sterling meticulously curated his collection, mixing legitimate pieces with carefully laundered artifacts from his stolen cache. He hired a small staff of art experts and administrators, all carefully vetted to ensure their discretion and loyalty. Each employee underwent extensive background checks and signed iron-clad non-disclosure agreements, with generous compensation packages ensuring their continued silence. The gallery quickly gained a reputation for its exclusive showings and rare acquisitions, drawing the attention of wealthy collectors and art enthusiasts from across the region. Sterling's keen eye for both authentic masterpieces and questionable treasures helped establish the Sterling Galleria as a must-visit destination for serious collectors, while his network of connections in the art world provided a steady stream of both legitimate and shadowy acquisitions to keep his displays fresh and intriguing.

But for Sterling, the true value of the gallery lay in its proximity to Grant. From his new vantage point, he could keep a close eye on his former colleague, tracking his movements and gathering intelligence on his activities through a network of informants and casual observers. Sterling often found himself standing at the gallery's front window, watching the passersby and wondering if today would be the day Grant would walk through his doors. He would trace his fingers along the cool glass, lost in memories of their shared past, while mentally cataloging every detail about his rival's routines, associates, and potential weaknesses. The gallery had become more than just a business venture - it was his personal watchtower, perfectly positioned to monitor the man who knew too much about their complicated history.

As the months passed, Sterling's network of contacts grew steadily, and he began to establish himself as a respected figure in the local art scene. He attended charity galas and hosted lavish openings at the Sterling Galleria, charming wealthy patrons with his encyclopedic knowledge of art history and refined tastes. Behind his carefully cultivated smile and polished demeanor, he kept his ear to the ground for any whisper of Grant or the artifacts they had once pursued together. Each new connection was meticulously vetted, each casual conversation analyzed for hidden meanings or potential leads that might bring him closer to his old rival. The social obligations were merely a means to an end - stepping stones in his relentless pursuit of unfinished business from their shared past.

Sterling's reputation in the art world grew exponentially, and with it, the Sterling Galleria's influence spread throughout international collecting circles. The gallery became a premier hub for elite collectors and discerning connoisseurs, its pristine walls adorned with priceless works that drew admiration and envy in equal measure. Private auctions and exclusive viewings attracted wealthy patrons from across continents, cementing the gallery's status as an epicenter of fine art trading. But beneath the polished veneer of legitimacy and sophistication, Sterling had woven an intricate web of illicit dealings, cultivating a shadow network of brokers and informants who operated in the murky waters between the legal art market and its criminal underbelly.

The gallery's back rooms became the stage for clandestine meetings and hushed negotiations, with deals sealed over rare cognac in leather-bound private chambers. Sterling's network of contacts expanded to include not just wealthy patrons, but also smugglers, forgers, and black market dealers who specialized in moving precious cargo across borders without scrutiny. He cultivated relationships with corrupt officials who could turn a blind eye to questionable provenance, greasing palms with both money and favors, and maintained a stable of skilled artisans who could create flawless reproductions of lost masterpieces. These craftsmen worked in secret studios, their expertise allowing Sterling to orchestrate elaborate schemes of substitution and deception that fooled even the most discerning collectors.

Sterling's expertise in identifying valuable artifacts, honed during his time with the Allied Art Recovery Task Force, proved invaluable in his new enterprise. He could spot a genuine piece among a sea of forgeries, and knew exactly how to market stolen goods to collectors who asked a few questions about origins. His trained eye could discern the subtle brushstrokes of a master painter from those of an imitator, detect the minute variations in patina that separated authentic bronze from modern reproductions, and evaluate the crystalline structure of precious gems that revealed their true age. This knowledge, combined with his understanding of the black market's inner workings, made him an unstoppable force in the underground art trade, capable of moving even the most notorious pieces through a labyrinth of false provenances and manufactured histories.

The gallery hosted exclusive, invitation-only events where select clients could view and purchase items that never appeared in public catalogs. These soirées were carefully orchestrated affairs, with Sterling personally vetting each attendee's background, connections, and financial resources. In these dimly lit, luxurious spaces, millions of dollars changed hands over glasses of vintage champagne and imported caviar, with Sterling taking a hefty cut of each transaction. The events were masterfully choreographed, from the strategic placement of security personnel disguised as waitstaff to the careful timing of when certain pieces were revealed to potential buyers. Sterling had perfected the art of discretion, ensuring that even the most questionable acquisitions could be sold without raising suspicions from authorities or legitimate dealers.

To maintain his cover, Sterling ensured that the gallery's public face remained impeccable. He donated generously to local charities, sponsored high-profile art restoration projects at prestigious museums, and even occasionally tipped off authorities about minor infractions in the art world to deflect suspicion from his own activities. His carefully cultivated image as a patron of the arts extended to hosting educational workshops for aspiring young artists and establishing scholarship funds at prominent art schools, all while using these legitimate enterprises to mask the true nature of his dealings. The press regularly praised his philanthropic efforts, never suspecting that these charitable works served as smoke screens for his darker pursuits in the shadowy corners of the art world.

As his illicit empire grew, Sterling became increasingly paranoid about security. He installed state-of-the-art surveillance systems throughout the gallery and employed a team of discreet security personnel, many of whom were former military operatives with unwavering loyalty to their employer. Hidden vaults were constructed within the building's walls, accessible only through a series of intricate security measures known only to Sterling himself. The vaults, reinforced with blast-proof steel and equipped with environmental controls to preserve delicate artifacts, were cleverly disguised behind rotating panels and false walls. Even his most trusted employees were kept in the dark about the full extent of these security measures, as Sterling compartmentalized information to ensure no single person could compromise his operation.

As time marched on, Sterling's fascination with the Amara Necklace morphed into a relentless obsession. He devoted innumerable hours to meticulously scrutinizing ancient records and photographs, hunting for the slightest hint that could guide him to its location. The recollection of that pivotal day in the cavern, when the necklace had been within his grasp, continued to torment his dreams and plague his waking thoughts.

His thirst for the elusive treasure drove him to seek out the expertise of historians, art collectors, and even those rumored to dabble in the dark arts. He left no stone unturned, scouring the most obscure corners of the art world in search of information. His once-thriving gallery began to suffer, as his focus shifted almost entirely to his quest for the Amara Necklace.

Unbeknownst to him, his desperate pursuit had not gone unnoticed. Whispers of his obsession echoed through the shadowy underbelly of the art world, attracting the attention of unsavory characters, who saw an opportunity to profit from his fixation. The stage was set for a dangerous game of cat and mouse, with the Amara Necklace as the ultimate prize.

Sterling's suspicions about Grant's involvement in the necklace's disappearance intensified with each passing day, gnawing at his thoughts until they consumed his every waking moment. He hired private investigators to track Grant's movements and monitor his communications, sparing no expense in his obsessive pursuit of the truth. Yet their reports always came back frustratingly inconclusive, filled with mundane details and dead-end leads that led nowhere. The lack of concrete evidence only fueled Sterling's paranoia and determination, pushing him to explore increasingly dangerous avenues of investigation. He began to see conspiracies in every shadow, convinced that Grant was always one step ahead, masterfully covering his tracks while the precious Amara Necklace slipped further from reach.

In the privacy of his office at the Sterling Galleria, he constructed an elaborate web of theories and connections on a large corkboard. Red strings crisscrossed between photographs, newspaper clippings, and handwritten notes, all centered around a sketch of the Amara Necklace. Sterling spent hours staring at this board, muttering to himself as he tried to piece together the puzzle, his fingers tracing the paths between each connection until the strings began to fray from his constant touch.

His obsession began to affect his business dealings. He became distracted during important meetings, his mind always wandering back to the necklace. Mid-conversation, his eyes would glaze over, fixating on some distant point as he mentally revisited his theories. Clients noticed his erratic behavior, and rumors began to circulate about his mental state. Several longtime patrons quietly took their business elsewhere, but Sterling paid no heed to the whispers; in his mind, nothing mattered more than reclaiming what he saw as rightfully his.

Sterling's search for the necklace led him to make increasingly risky decisions. He began to leverage his connections in the black market, putting out discreet feelers for any information about the Amara Necklace or Grant's activities. He offered exorbitant sums for even the smallest lead, jeopardizing the gallery's legitimate operations. His contacts grew seedier, his meetings more clandestine, often taking place in dimly lit back rooms of questionable establishments where reputations meant nothing and money talked. The prestigious Sterling name, once synonymous with fine art and culture, was beginning to carry a different weight in certain circles.

Chapter Ten

As the years passed, James Grant found himself unable to shake the weight of the Amara Necklace's secret. The artifact, hidden away in a secure location known only to him, haunted his conscience like a persistent demon. He knew he couldn't keep it forever, but returning it posed significant risks, not just to himself, but to those who might become entangled in its complex history.

Grant began a meticulous investigation into the necklace's origins, determined to find its rightful owners and perhaps, in doing so, absolve himself of the guilt that had plagued him for years. He spent countless hours poring over historical documents, tracing genealogies, and reaching out to discrete contacts in the art world. His inquiries were cautious and calculated, never revealing the necklace's location or his possession of it, always dancing around the truth with carefully chosen words and half-truths. He knew Sterling had moved to town and opened an art galleria, most likely to pursue the necklace. Even though he and Sterling stayed at arm's length, James knew that Sterling suspected him of having the necklace. Each would keep tabs on the other through business contacts and dealings.

Meanwhile, in the offices of the Sterling Galleria, Nikolai Sterling's network of informants buzzed with activity like a hive of industrious bees. A whisper here, a rumor there - all pointing to Grant's clandestine search. Sterling's eyes gleamed with a mixture of triumph and fury as the pieces fell into place, a puzzle he had been trying to solve for more than fifteen years, finally taking shape before him.

One evening, as Sterling sat behind his imposing mahogany desk, his most trusted black market contact slipped into the room like a shadow. The man, a nervous fellow with darting eyes and fidgeting hands, leaned in close, his breath carrying the faint scent of cigarettes and fear.

"It's confirmed, Mr. Sterling. Grant has the necklace. He's been asking around, trying to trace its lineage. He's been careful, but not careful enough."

Sterling's fingers tightened on the arms of his chair, the leather creaking under his grip. "And the owners? Has he made any progress there?"

"No luck yet. But he's getting close. Word is he's made contact with some European historians specializing in Nazi-looted art. They're digging deep into records that haven't seen the light of day in decades."

Sterling dismissed the informant with a wave, his mind racing with possibilities and threats. Grant's efforts to return the necklace threatened to undermine his lifelong dream of having all seven pieces to uncover untold wealth somewhere in the heart of Germany. The Amara Necklace was more than just a valuable artifact - it was the key to unlocking secrets Sterling had spent decades pursuing, secrets that could reshape the landscape of the art world and beyond.

He stood, pacing the length of his office, his footsteps muffled by the plush carpet. Grant's moral compass had always been a thorn in his side, a constant reminder of the path Sterling had chosen not to take. But this... this was unthinkable. It was a direct threat to everything Sterling had been after, everything he had sacrificed for. He had to act fast, to intercept Grant before he could succeed in his mission. The stakes were too high, the potential losses too great to allow Grant's misguided sense of righteousness to prevail.

Sterling paced his office, his mind churning with possibilities. He knew he had to act swiftly to intercept Grant before the necklace slipped through his fingers once again. A plan began to form, as intricate and delicate as the craftsmanship work on the Amara Necklace itself.

He requested his most trusted associate, a master forger named Anton. "I need documents," Sterling said, his voice low and intense. "Flawless ones. We're creating a family with a claim to the Amara Necklace."

Anton nodded, understanding the gravity of the request. "It'll take time, but I can do it. How far back do you need the lineage?"

"All the way to the 18th century. Make it ironclad."

For the next week, Sterling and Anton worked tirelessly, crafting a believable backstory for a fictional family. They created birth certificates, marriage records, and even fabricated journal entries detailing the necklace's journey through generations.

With the groundwork laid, Anton reached out to his network of informants, spreading whispers about a family seeking a long-lost heirloom. He knew the art world was small, and news traveled fast. It wouldn't be long before Grant caught wind of it.

Sure enough, within weeks, Sterling received word that Grant was making discreet inquiries about the forged family. It was time to set the trap.

Sterling arranged for a chance encounter between Anton and Grant at an exclusive art auction. As they stood examining a rare Rembrandt, Anton struck up a conversation, carefully steering it towards the topic of lost artifacts.

"I've heard rumors," Anton said casually, "of a family searching for a necklace. Something quite valuable, I believe. Perhaps you've heard of it?"

Grant's eyes widened slightly, his interest piqued. "I may have. The Amara Necklace, by any chance?"

Anton nodded, feigning surprise. "Yes, that's the one. I represent the family in question. They've been searching for it for generations."

Grant studied Anton's face, searching for any sign of deception. "I'd be interested in speaking with the family," he said carefully. "To verify their claim, of course. I might be able to assist them in its recovery."

"Of course," Sterling replied smoothly. "I can arrange a meeting. They're quite eager to recover their heritage."

As they exchanged contact information and Anton promised to be in touch soon with proof of the family's claim. Sterling, after hearing the recounting of the encounter, could barely contain his excitement. The bait was set, and Grant had taken it. Now, all he had to do was reel him in.

A few days after the auction, Grant sat in his study at Hawthorn Manor, surrounded by stacks of books and papers. The phone rang, breaking the silence. He picked it up, recognizing Anton's voice on the other end.

"Mr. Grant, I hope I'm not disturbing you," Anton said smoothly. "I have some news regarding the matter we discussed at the auction."

Grant's pulse quickened. "Go on," he replied, trying to keep his voice neutral.

"The family I represent has agreed for you to inspect the family records. They are quite private and ask that I handle the meeting for the inspection. Once you are satisfied, a final meeting can be scheduled for delivery. They've gathered quite an extensive collection of documents detailing their claim to the Amara Necklace. Would you be interested in reviewing them?"

Grant paused, weighing his options. He knew he had to tread carefully, but his curiosity was overwhelming. "Yes, I would. When and where can we meet?"

"Does tomorrow afternoon work? How about the public library on 4th Street? Say, 3 PM? It's a neutral location, and they have a private room we can use for discretion."

Grant hesitated. The public library wasn't his first choice, but he couldn't let this opportunity slip away. "Very well," he agreed. "I'll be there."

"Excellent," Anton replied. "I'll bring all the necessary documentation. I think you'll find it quite... illuminating."

As Grant hung up the phone, he couldn't shake a feeling of unease. He knew he was walking into potentially dangerous territory, but putting this necklace back into the hands it belonged to was too strong to resist... not to mention the weight that would be lifted off his shoulders.

Grant arrived at the public library precisely at 3 PM, his briefcase filled with reference notes and research, clutched tightly in his hand. He scanned the lobby, spotting Anton near the reference desk. The two men exchanged nods and made their way to a private study room.

Once inside, Anton spread out a collection of documents on the table. Grant's eyes widened as he took in the array of yellowed papers, photographs, and leather-bound journals.

"As you can see," Anton began, "the family's claim to the Amara Necklace is quite extensive."

Grant leaned in, examining a faded photograph of a woman wearing what appeared to be the necklace. He picked up a nearby document, a birth certificate dated 1892.

"May I?" Grant asked, reaching for a pair of white cotton gloves from his briefcase.

Anton nodded, watching intently as Grant meticulously inspected each item. The forger's work was impeccable, with every detail crafted to withstand scrutiny.

Grant pored over family trees, letters, and even a handwritten account of the necklace's journey through generations. His brow furrowed in concentration as he cross-referenced dates and names.

After nearly two hours of examination, Grant sat back in his chair, a look of resignation on his face. "These appear to be in order," he said quietly. "The family's claim seems legitimate."

Anton leaned forward, his eyes gleaming. "Then I assume you have the necklace and will return it to the family?"

Grant nodded slowly. "Yes, I believe it's the right thing to do. We can arrange the handover for next week. I'll need time to retrieve it from a secured location."

"Of course," Anton replied smoothly. "The family will be overjoyed to have their heirloom returned. Shall we say next Wednesday, same time? That should give the family enough time to come to the States for the exchange."

"That would be fine," Grant agreed, standing up to shake Anton's hand.

As they parted ways outside the library, Grant couldn't shake a nagging feeling in the pit of his stomach. But he pushed it aside, convinced he was doing the right thing by returning the necklace to its rightful owners.

Grant stood before a false bookcase in the library of Hawthorn Manor. His heart raced with anticipation as he carefully pulled the bookcase open, revealing the secret entrance. He quietly entered the tunnel, his footsteps quick, and gently closed the bookcase behind him. It was as if he had just disappeared from the library, leaving no trace of his presence. The air grew cooler and humid as he slowly walked down the darkened stairs, his hand trailing along the damp stone wall for support.

His fingers trembled slightly as he placed the old brass key into the lock of the massive wooden door, its intricate carvings barely visible in the dim light. With a final turn of the handle, accompanied by the groaning of ancient hinges, the door swung open. It revealed a musty cavern filled with antiques and shelves lined with various artifacts and documents, each item holding its own story and secrets. The air was thick with the scent of aged paper and polished wood, a testament to the history contained within this hidden chamber.

His eyes scanned the contents until they landed on a small, ornate box tucked away in the corner. Grant reached for it, feeling the weight of history in his hands. He carefully opened the lid, revealing the Amara Necklace nestled within.

The sapphire at its center seemed to pulse with an inner light, its deep blue hue as captivating as the day he first laid eyes on it in that hidden Nazi cache. Grant lifted the necklace gently, allowing the gold chain to slip through his fingers.

He carried it to an open spot on a desk, where his journal lay open. With reverent care, he placed the necklace on a soft cloth and began to sketch. His pencil moved swiftly across the page, capturing the intricate work of the chain and the perfect setting of the sapphire.

As he drew, Grant found himself lost in memories of that fateful day in the Harz Mountains. The tension with Sterling, the weight of the discovery, and the decision that had led him to this moment all came flooding back. he drew a snake encompassing the Safire as a reminder of the dangerous path it had taken throughout history. Something only he would understand.

His sketch complete, Grant added notes in the margins, detailing the necklace's dimensions and unique features. He paid special attention to the hidden compartment on the back of the clasp, making sure to document the coded numbers engraved within.

With a heavy sigh, Grant closed his journal and carefully returned the Amara Necklace to its box. As he locked it away in the vault once more, he couldn't shake the feeling that this might be the last time he saw it.

The following day, Grant met Anton at the library as agreed. Anton ushered him into the private room and closed the door behind him, locking it. The soft click of the lock echoed in the silent room, sending a chill down Grant's spine.

"I hope you don't mind the precaution," Anton said smoothly, gesturing for Grant to take a seat. "We wouldn't want any interruptions during such a delicate exchange. The family should be here shortly."

Grant nodded, his hand instinctively tightening on the briefcase containing the Amara Necklace. He scanned the room, noting the absence of windows and the single door behind Anton. The air felt thick with tension.

"While we wait, may I see the documents once more?" Grant asked, trying to keep his voice steady.

Anton half smiled, nervously reaching into his own briefcase. "Of course, I have everything here."

As Anton spread the papers across the table, Grant couldn't shake the feeling that something was off. The room seemed to shrink around him, the walls closing in. He forced himself to focus on the documents before him, double-checking the details he had memorized from their previous meeting.

"I must say, Mr. Grant," Anton began, his tone casual but with an undercurrent of something darker, "you've been quite thorough in your examination of our claim. One might almost think you had a personal stake in this matter."

Grant's head snapped up, meeting Anton's gaze. The man's eyes were cold, calculating, and utterly devoid of the warmth they had shown in previous encounters.

"I simply wanted to ensure everything was in order," Grant replied carefully. "The Amara Necklace is a significant piece of history. It's important that it ends up in the right hands."

Anton leaned back in his chair, a smirk playing at the corners of his mouth. "Indeed it is, Mr. Grant. Indeed it is."

A sharp knock at the door cut through the tension in the room. Anton's eyes flickered to Grant for a moment before he moved to answer it.

"It seems our family has arrived," Anton said in a playful manner. As the door swung open, Grant's blood ran cold. Nikolai Sterling strode into the room, his face a mask of triumph.

Grant leapt to his feet, his chair clattering to the floor behind him. "Nikolai! What the hell is this?"

Sterling slowly approached James and placed his hands on his shoulders and proceeded to kiss him on both cheeks. James stood frozen in shock. Sterling's lips curled into a smirk. "Come now, James. Surely you didn't think you could keep the Amara Necklace from me forever?" as he took a few steps back.

Fury and betrayal coursed through Grant's veins. He lunged forward, fists clenched, but froze as he heard the unmistakable click of a gun being cocked. Anton had produced a pistol from his jacket and now held it steadily trained on Grant.

"I wouldn't do anything rash if I were you, Mr. Grant," Sterling said coldly.

Grant's mind raced, piecing together the elaborate deception. The forged documents, the staged meetings, the false family claim - it had all been a ruse to lure him here.

"You bastard," Grant snapped at Sterling. "You've been after the necklace all this time."

Sterling circled the table, his eyes never leaving the briefcase that held the precious artifact. "I knew it was you that stole it that night. Did you really think I'd let it go so easily? That I'd forget about the secret it holds?"

Grant's hands clenched at his sides, helpless rage building within him. He'd walked right into their trap, blinded by his own desire to do the right thing. Now, he stood cornered in a locked room, with a gun pointed at his chest and his oldest enemy mere feet away from claiming the very treasure he'd sworn to protect.

Sterling moved swiftly to the briefcase, his eyes gleaming with anticipation. With deft fingers, he unlatched it and reached inside, pulling out the ornate box that housed the Amara Necklace. Grant watched helplessly as Sterling opened the lid, his breath catching as the sapphire caught the light.

Holding the necklace up, Sterling examined it closely, turning it over in his hands. He ran his fingers along the intricate lattice work, checked the clasp, and even peered at the hidden compartment on the back of the pendant. A slow smile spread across his face as he confirmed its authenticity.

"Exquisite," Sterling murmured, more to himself than anyone else in the room. "It's even more beautiful than I remembered."

Satisfied that he held the genuine article, Sterling carefully returned the necklace to its box and tucked it into his own jacket pocket. He turned to Anton, who still held the gun trained on Grant.

"Make sure no one finds him," Sterling instructed, his voice cold and businesslike. "I don't want any loose ends."

Anton nodded, his grip on the pistol never wavering. "Consider it done."

With one last triumphant look at Grant, Sterling strode towards the door. He paused for a moment, his hand on the handle, and turned back to face his longtime rival.

"I'm sorry, James, we could have done this together. It's been a pleasure doing business with you," Sterling said, his tone dripping with sarcasm. "Don't beat yourself up about this. It was only a matter of time before you slipped up. Do Svidaniya old friend."

And with that, Sterling slipped out of the room, the soft click of the door closing behind him echoing like a cannon in Grant's ears. Grant was left alone with Anton, his mind racing to find a way out of this desperate situation.

Anton gestured with the gun, motioning for Grant to move. "Let's go for a little drive, shall we?" he said, his voice low and menacing. "And don't try anything stupid. We're going to walk out of here nice and casual, like two colleagues finishing up a meeting."

Grant slowly rose to his feet, his mind frantically searching for a way out of this situation. He knew he couldn't risk making a scene in the library - too many innocent bystanders could get hurt.

"Hands where I can see them," Anton instructed. "Now, walk in front of me. Act natural."

Grant complied, his shoulders tense as he felt the barrel of the gun pressed against his back. They made their way out of the private room and through the library's main area. Grant's eyes darted around, looking for any opportunity to signal for help, but Anton kept him moving steadily towards the exit.

As they stepped out into the afternoon sun, Anton directed Grant towards a nondescript sedan parked at the curb. "Get in the passenger seat," he ordered. "And remember, one wrong move and things will get very messy for you."

Grant's hand hesitated on the car door handle, his survival instincts screaming at him to run. But with the gun still trained on him and pedestrians milling about nearby, he knew he had no choice but to comply. He opened the door and slid into the passenger seat, his mind racing to formulate a plan as Anton moved around to the driver's side.

As Anton navigated the car through the city streets, Grant's eyes darted constantly, searching for any opportunity to escape. The gun remained pointed at him, a constant reminder of the danger he was in. The bustling city gradually gave way to less populated areas as they approached the outskirts.

Grant's heart raced as he recognized they were nearing a bridge. He knew this might be his last chance to act. As the car began to ascend the gentle slope of the bridge, Grant's muscles tensed, preparing for action.

Just as they reached the midpoint of the bridge, Grant made his move. With lightning speed, he lunged across the center console, grabbing the steering wheel with both hands. Anton let out a startled yell, his finger instinctively tightening on the trigger. The gun went off, the bullet shattering the passenger side window.

Grant wrenched the wheel hard to the right, using all his strength to overpower Anton. The car swerved violently, tires screeching against the pavement. Anton struggled to regain control, but Grant's sudden attack had caught him off guard.

In a matter of seconds, the car careened towards the side of the bridge. Grant braced himself as the vehicle slammed into one of the concrete support columns with a deafening crash. The impact sent shockwaves through the car, crinkling the metal with explosive force.

For a moment, everything went silent. Then, the sound of twisting metal and shattering glass filled the air as the crumpled car settled into its final position. Smoke began to rise from the mangled hood, and the acrid smell of burnt rubber permeated the air.

Inside the mangled wreckage of the car, Anton's body lay motionless, his neck having been brutally snapped by the sheer force of face hitting the steering wheel. The once-formidable man was now nothing more than a lifeless shell, his plans and ambitions extinguished in an instant. As Grant slipped in and out of consciousness, his head throbbing and vision blurring, he could hear the urgent voices of approaching bystanders and the piercing wail of sirens in the distance. The sound grew steadily louder, cutting through the eerie silence that had fallen over the crash site. Grant's mind struggled to process the surrounding chaos, his thoughts a jumbled mess of pain, confusion, and the dawning realization of what had just transpired.

Chapter Eleven

Grant sat in his study at Hawthorn Manor, his arm still in a sling and a fading bruise on his temple. The past few weeks had been a blur of hospital visits, police interviews, and painful recovery. He stared out the window, watching the spring leaves dance in the breeze, lost in thought about the events that had led to the crash.

A gentle knock on the door broke his trance. Evelyn entered, carrying a tray with hot tea and buttered bread.

"How are you feeling today, dear?" she asked, setting the tray down on the side table.

Grant managed a weak smile. "Better, I suppose. Still sore, but the doctor says I'm healing well."

Evelyn poured him a cup of tea, her hands trembling slightly. "The police called earlier. They've concluded their investigation."

Grant's eyebrows raised. "And?"

"They're ruling it an accident," Evelyn said, her voice barely above a whisper. "They believe the driver lost control of the vehicle."

Grant let out a long, slow breath. Part of him was relieved - he wouldn't have to explain the truth about

Anton, Sterling, or the necklace. But another part of him felt uneasy about the lie.

"That's... good news, I suppose," he said carefully.

Evelyn nodded, but her eyes were filled with concern. "James, what really happened that day? You've been so quiet about it all."

Grant took a sip of tea, wincing as the movement jostled his injured arm. He looked at his younger wife, seeing the worry etched on her face. He wanted to tell her everything - about Sterling's betrayal, the forged documents, Anton's threats. But he knew the truth would only lead to more questions that he didn't want to answer.

"It happened so fast, Evie," he said, opting for a partial truth. "One moment we were driving, the next... chaos. I'm just grateful to have made it out alive."

Evelyn reached out and squeezed his hand gently. "We all are, James. We all are."

A few minutes after Evelyn left, another knock sounded at the study door. Grant called for the visitor to enter, and Albert Carlisle stepped inside, his usually jovial face creased with concern.

Albert pulled up a chair next to James's desk, his tweed jacket rustling as he settled in. Though only in his thirties, he carried himself with the measured grace of someone well-versed in the delicate world of fine art and antiquities.

"Quite a scare you gave us, old friend," Albert said, loosening his tie.

James studied the younger man's face. Over the past five years, their relationship had evolved from casual acquaintances to a deep personal bond. Albert's keen eye for authenticity and had impressed James at their first meeting at an east coast auction house.

"You should have seen the other fellow," James attempted a joke, but Albert's expression remained serious.

"I've been managing your accounts while you were... indisposed," Albert said. "Made sure everything stayed above board, just as you taught me."

James nodded appreciatively. He'd spent countless hours teaching Albert the intricacies of art authentication, the complex web of international buyers, and most importantly, using Albert to offload some of the treasure whose families no longer existed thanks for evilness of the Third Reich. Although Albert owned a little antique shop, he brokered deals all over the world. Albert even did business with the Sterling Galleria for consignment of items that were to be auctioned. Afterall, the Sterling Galleria was the only game in town when it came to high dollar auctions.

"You've learned well, Bertie," James said, using the nickname he'd given the younger man. "Better than I could have hoped when I first took you under my wing."

Albert's shoulders straightened at the praise. Their mentorship had started gradually, a shared cup of coffee here, a consultation there. But James had recognized something of himself in the younger man's passionate pursuit of artistic truth, his determination to preserve history rather than merely profit from it.

"I had a good teacher," Albert replied, his voice carrying a hint of pride. "Though I doubt I'll ever match your expertise in German Expressionism."

James chuckled, remembering the hours they'd spent poring over auction catalogs, discussing brush techniques, and debating the authenticity of various pieces. Albert had become more than just a protégé - he'd become a trusted friend and confidant in a world where such relationships were rare.

"How are you holding up?" Albert asked, settling into the armchair across from Grant.

Grant sighed, setting down his teacup. "I've been better, Albert. But I suppose I should be grateful things weren't worse."

Albert nodded solemnly. "Indeed. Look, James, I hate to pry, but something about this whole affair doesn't sit right with me. Is there anything you'd like to tell me? Anything at all?"

Grant studied his young friend's face for a long moment. The weight of secrets pressed heavily on his chest, and suddenly, he found himself longing to unburden himself to someone he trusted.

"Actually, Albert, there is," Grant said quietly. He leaned forward, wincing slightly at the movement. "Close the door please. What I'm about to tell you must remain between us."

Albert's eyebrows rose, but he nodded in agreement as he walked through the door to the study and closed it softly.

Grant took a deep breath and began to recount the true events leading up to the crash. He told Albert about the necklace, its origins, what secrets the necklace holds, and Sterling's betrayal. He explained his role in the AARTF and his connection to Sterling. Albert sat is disbelief.

As Grant spoke, Albert's expression shifted from surprise to shock to grave understanding. When Grant finished, a heavy silence fell over the study.

Finally, Albert spoke, his voice barely above a whisper. "My God, James. I had no idea. All these years, and you've been carrying this burden alone." He paused, collecting his thoughts before continuing. "What do you plan to do now? Do you think Nikolai even has it anymore? He's probably already sold it off to some wealthy collector or hidden it away in some remote location."

Grant shook his head wearily, the weight of his secrets evident in the slump of his shoulders. "I don't think so, Albert. The necklace isn't just a simple piece of jewelry—it's part of a pretty complicated puzzle, a key to something far greater. If Nikolai still has the other six pieces, it would probably take him a few months, maybe even years, to figure out how they all fit together. He's still thinks like a soldier, not a code breaker. The Germans had some of the best minds in Europe. Like the Enigma, it is more than likely going to take a team of smart people to figure it out." He leaned forward, his eyes intense. "The Amara Necklace and its six counterparts could lead to a treasure cache worth millions... hundreds of millions, perhaps even billions, in today's market. Priceless artifacts, lost works of art, gold. They looted antiquities from all four corners of the globe. They had a real niche for religious artifacts—who knows what's truly hidden away? I can promise you, Albert, it's not for sale. Nikolai wouldn't dare part with it, not when he's so close to unlocking the location of that vault."

Albert leaned forward, his brow furrowed in thought. After a moment, he spoke in a hushed tone, "James, if this necklace is truly as important as you say, perhaps we should consider... retrieving it ourselves."

Grant's eyebrows shot up in surprise. He hadn't expected such a bold suggestion from his usually cautious friend. The idea was tempting, but fraught with danger.

"You mean steal it back?" Grant asked, his voice low.

Albert nodded, a glimmer of excitement in his eyes. "Precisely! We have the advantage of inside knowledge. I have several pieces of art sitting in the Galleria's vault awaiting the next auction. I've seen the inner layout of the Galleria. Plus, with your connections, we might could just pull it off."

Grant leaned back in his chair, wincing slightly as he adjusted his injured arm. He stared out the window, considering the proposition. The risks were enormous - if caught, they could face severe legal consequences, not to mention the potential wrath of Sterling and his associates.

But the thought of the necklace in the wrong hands, the secrets it held potentially being used for nefarious purposes, gnawed at him. Could he live with himself if he didn't at least try to recover it?

"It's a dangerous game you're proposing, Albert," Grant said slowly, turning back to his friend. "We'd be risking everything - our reputations, our freedom, possibly even our lives."

Albert nodded gravely. "I understand the risks, James. But sometimes, the right thing to do isn't the safe thing."

Grant fell silent again, weighing the options in his mind. The rational part of him screamed that it was madness, but another part - the reason that he had joined the AARTF in the first place - whispered that it might be their only choice.

"Let's say we did attempt this," Grant said carefully. "Where would we even begin?"

Albert's eyes lit up, realizing that Grant was seriously considering the idea. "Well, first we'd need to gather lots intelligence. Find out where the necklace is being kept, what kind of security we're dealing with..."

As Albert began to outline a rough plan, Grant found himself both terrified and exhilarated by the prospect. It was reckless, potentially disastrous, but it also offered a chance at redemption - a way to right the wrongs that had led to this moment.

Chapter Twelve

On the evening of June 12, 1963, James Grant and Albert Carlisle sat in a nondescript car parked across the street from the Sterling Galleria. The elegant façade of the building loomed before them, its windows dark save for the security lights that cast eerie shadows on the cobblestone street.

James checked his watch for the third time in as many minutes. "It's almost time," he murmured, his voice tight with tension.

Albert nodded, his eyes never leaving the gallery's entrance. "Are you sure about this, James? There's still time to back out."

James shook his head firmly, his weathered features set with determination. "We've come too far to turn back now. The Amara Necklace doesn't belong to Sterling, and you know as well as I do what he will do with it. The black market would be inundated with relics. The world would never see them again, not to mention the owners." His fingers drummed against the steering wheel as memories of similar operations during the war flooded back - the desperate race to save priceless artifacts before they vanished into private collections forever.

The two men had spent months meticulously planning this heist. Through careful observation and a network of contacts, they had pieced together the gaps in the gallery's security measures, staff schedules, and most importantly, the location of the vault where Sterling kept his most valuable acquisitions. James had forked out lots of money to gather the intel.

Albert reached into his coat pocket, feeling the weight of the small leather case containing their lock-picking tools, and pulled them out. James noticed and his heart raced as he thought about what they were about to attempt. Breaking into the Sterling Galleria was no small feat—the security systems were state-of-the-art for their time, and Sterling's reputation for dealing with thieves was notoriously brutal.

"Remember the plan," Albert said, his voice barely above a whisper. "We have a fifteen-minute window when the night guard makes his rounds. Any longer, and we risk tripping the silent alarm."

James nodded, taking a deep breath to steady his nerves. They had rehearsed this plan countless times, but the reality of what they were about to do was finally sinking in. If they were caught, the consequences would be severe. But the thought of the Amara Necklace—and the secrets it held—falling into the wrong hands steeled his resolve. In his mind he knew it was illegal, but the sometimes doing the right thing was the legal thing to do.

As the clock struck midnight, James saw the night guard emerge from the gallery's side entrance, right on schedule. He gave Albert a quick nod, and they silently exited the car, blending into the shadows as they approached the building.

James and Albert moved swiftly across the street, their footsteps barely audible on the cobblestone. As they reached the side entrance of the Sterling Galleria, James pulled out the leather case and selected a slender pick. With practiced hands, he worked the lock while Albert kept watch. Albert slipped a long blade between the top of the door and the frame, moved it side to side. When we were sure the door alarm had been cut, he worked on the door with both hands.

The lock clicked open, and they slipped inside. The gallery's interior was eerily quiet, filled with shadows cast by the dim security lights. James led the way, his eyes adjusting to the darkness as they navigated through the main exhibition hall.

"This way," Albert whispered, gesturing towards a corridor that led to the back offices.

They moved cautiously, aware that any misstep could trigger an alarm. As they approached Sterling's office, James felt his pulse quicken. He knew the vault was hidden behind a false panel in the wall, concealed by an ornate painting.

Albert cupped his ear to the door, listening for any sign of movement inside. "Coast is clear," he murmured.

James and Albert picked the lock and entered the office and made their way to the painting. James carefully removed it from the wall, revealing the sleek metal surface of the vault. This was the moment of truth—the lock on this wall safe was more sophisticated than the simple deadbolt on the side entrance.

Albert pulled out a well-worn stethoscope from his coat pocket and delicately placed it against the vault's cool, metallic surface. With practiced hands, he began turning the dial with painstaking precision, his fingers moving in minute increments. Each click of the intricate mechanism echoed loudly in the silent room, reverberating off the walls and making James wince involuntarily. The tension in the air was palpable as both men held their breath, acutely aware of how much was riding on Albert's expertise.

James, unable to contain his curiosity and nervous energy, leaned in close and whispered, "How on earth do you know how to do this? Actually, never mind. I don't want to know." His voice was a mix of awe and trepidation, betraying both his admiration for Albert's skills and his unease about their origins. Albert, without missing a beat in his delicate work, slightly turned his head towards James and offered a mischievous wink. The gesture spoke volumes, hinting at a colorful past filled with secrets that James could only imagine.

After what felt like an eternity, the vault door swung open. James reached inside, his hand closing around a small wooden box. He opened it, and there it was—the Amara Necklace, its sapphire gleaming even in the near darkness.

"We've got it," James breathed, a mixture of relief and triumph washing over him.

Albert walked to the doorway, his face tense. "Time to go. The guard will be back any second."

James nodded, carefully tucking the box into his inner pocket. They retraced their steps, moving swiftly but silently through the gallery. As they reached the side entrance, they heard footsteps approaching from around the corner.

James and Albert froze, their hearts pounding in their chests. The footsteps grew louder, echoing off the gallery's marble floors. James quickly scanned their surroundings, his eyes landing on a small alcove partially hidden by a large sculpture.

"This way," he mouthed to Albert, gesturing towards the hiding spot.

The two men silently slipped into the alcove, pressing themselves against the wall, with Albert sliding into position beside him. James could feel the cool surface of the Amara Necklace through his jacket pocket, a stark reminder of what was at stake.

The night guard rounded the corner, his flashlight beam sweeping across the gallery floor. James held his breath, acutely aware of how exposed they were. If the guard decided to investigate the alcove, they would be discovered instantly.

Seconds stretched into an eternity as the guard paused, his light lingering near their hiding spot. James could see Albert's hand inching towards his pocket, where James knew he kept a small caliber pistol—a last resort they had hoped not to use. James put his hand on

Albert's arm and they met eyes. James gave a disapproving sideways nod.

Just as the tension reached its breaking point, the guard's radio crackled to life. "YA dumayu u nas neispraven datchik."

The guard grunted in acknowledgment and turned away, his footsteps receding down the corridor. James and Albert remained still for several more moments, ensuring the coast was clear before they dared to move.

"That was too close," Albert whispered, his voice barely audible.

James nodded, his pulse still racing. "Let's get out of here before our luck runs out."

They emerged from their hiding spot and made their way to the side entrance. Albert carefully disabled the door alarm and James carefully opened the door, peering out into the night. The back alley and street were deserted, bathed in the warm glow of streetlamps.

As they stepped out into the cool night air, a sense of accomplishment washed over them. They had done it—they had retrieved the Amara Necklace. But James knew their mission was far from over. Now came the challenge of keeping it out of Sterling's hands again and ensure it reached the right hands.

With one last glance at the Sterling Galleria, James and Albert disappeared into the shadows.

Chapter Thirteen

Sterling strode into his office the next morning, his confident gait faltering as he noticed immediately something amiss. The painting was off the wall, and the safe door hung open, its contents disturbed. His eyes widened in disbelief as he realized the necklace was gone.

Fury rose within him, his face flushing red as he clenched his fists. He paced the room, mind racing. Grant's face flashed in his thoughts - could he have done this? Sterling shook his head, struggling to reconcile the idea of Grant pulling off such a brazen heist at his age. And yet, heavy suspicion gnawed at him.

He ran a hand through his thinning hair, jaw clenched as he surveyed the scene. Sterling's mind whirled with questions and accusations, but one thing was certain - he would get to the bottom of this, no matter the cost.

Sterling paced his office, his polished shoes clicking rhythmically on the hardwood floor as his mind raced with possibilities. The loss of the Amara Necklace was a devastating blow, but he refused to let it be his undoing. A plan began to form in his mind, a cunning scheme that could potentially turn this setback into a lucrative windfall.

He picked up the phone, his fingers trembling slightly as he dialed a number he rarely used. "Vlad, I need your expertise. Tonight," he said tersely, his voice barely above a whisper.

As darkness fell over the city, Sterling met Vlad in the dimly lit alley behind the gallery. The burly man's scarred face remained impassive as Sterling outlined his audacious plan, his eyes darting occasionally to check for any unwanted observers.

"We're going to stage a heist. A big one. I want you to clear out the vault, take everything of value. Make it look convincing," Sterling explained, his voice a mixture of excitement and apprehension. "Leave no stone unturned."

Ivan nodded, his eyes glinting with understanding and a hint of eagerness. "And the security system?" he inquired, his deep voice rumbling in the quiet alley.

"Someone has already disabled both side entrances. The rest, I'll disable myself," Sterling assured him, a cold smile playing on his lips. "Just make sure you leave enough evidence to satisfy the police. We need this to look like a professional job, not an inside job."

Under cover of night, Sterling and Vlad executed their meticulously crafted plan with surgical precision. They methodically emptied the gallery's vault, their gloved hands carefully removing each valuable piece and replacing it with an eerie emptiness. As they worked, they painstakingly staged signs of more forced entries, from shattered glass to pried-open doors. Sterling, ever the perfectionist, even went so far as to rough himself up, creating bruises and cuts that would lend credibility to his story of a violent encounter.

As the first rays of dawn broke over the city skyline, Sterling stood outside the gallery, his disheveled appearance and convincingly distraught demeanor drawing concerned glances from passersby. He spoke to the police officers, his voice trembling with feigned shock and distress as he recounted a harrowing tale of masked intruders and a daring robbery. His performance was so compelling, so rich with detail and emotion, that it would have been worthy of a standing ovation on any stage. With an air of desperation, he insisted that the investigators fingerprint everything in his office, including the now-empty safe concealed behind an innocuous painting. His eyes, brimming with unshed tears, conveyed a burning desire to uncover the identity of the culprits who had stolen the priceless Amara necklace from his possession, all while inwardly reveling in the brilliance of his deception.

In the days that followed, Sterling masterfully played the part of the distraught victim to absolute perfection. He meticulously filed insurance claims, his hands trembling with feigned distress as he detailed each stolen item. He gave impassioned interviews to the eager press, his voice cracking with emotion as he recounted the devastating loss to his prized collection. Sterling even went so far as to dramatically vow to rebuild his collection, no matter the cost or time required. His performance was so convincing that even hardened investigators found themselves sympathizing with the seemingly broken man.

All the while, behind the scenes, Vlad worked tirelessly and with ruthless efficiency to sell the stolen goods on the shadowy black market. He navigated treacherous deals with dangerous buyers, always staying one step ahead of law enforcement. The ill-gotten profits from these transactions were then funneled back to Sterling through an intricate and bewildering labyrinth of offshore accounts, shell companies, and untraceable exchanges. The complexity of their financial web was a testament to Sterling's meticulous planning and Vlad's criminal expertise, ensuring that their elaborate scheme remained hidden from even the most discerning eyes.

James Grant leaned against the worn leather armchair in Albert's cluttered antique shop, his eyes darting nervously to the windows. The weight of their recent heist hung heavy in the air, mingling with the musty scent of old books and polished wood.

"Albert, I need you to keep the necklace," James said, his voice barely above a whisper. "Sterling's bound to come sniffing around Hawthorn Manor, and I can't risk him finding it there."

Albert's eyebrows shot up, his face creasing with concern. "Are you sure, James? That's quite a responsibility."

James nodded grimly. "I trust you. You know how to keep things hidden, and your shop's the last place Sterling would think to look." He glanced around in a less than favorable look.

Albert stroked his chin thoughtfully, his eyes gleaming with apprehension. "Alright, then. I'll keep it safe until this blows over. But what's your plan?"

"lie low for now," James replied, running a hand through his graying hair. "Act normal, tend to the estate. If Sterling comes around, I'll play dumb. He can't prove anything without the necklace. I'll threaten him with going to the authorities with his real identity. That's why he has never made a move on me, at least overtly."

Albert carefully wrapped the Amara Necklace in a soft cloth, his fingers treating it with reverence. He shuffled to the back of his shop, disappearing behind a beaded curtain. James heard the faint sound of creaking floorboards and the muffled thud of a hidden compartment closing.

When Albert returned, his face was set with determination. "It's done. Not even I could find it now if I didn't know where to look."

James exhaled slowly, feeling a weight lift from his shoulders. "Thank you, Albert. I owe you one."

"Just be careful, James," Albert warned, his green eyes sharp with concern. "Sterling's not a man to be messed with. He won't let this go easily."

James leaned back in the armchair, Albert's warning echoing in his mind. The gravity of the situation settled over him like a heavy cloak. He ran a hand through his hair, his brow furrowed in deep thought.

"You're right, Albert," James said after a long pause. "Sterling's not one to give up easily. We need to be prepared for anything."

Albert nodded solemnly, his eyes fixed on his old friend.

James leaned forward, his voice low and urgent. "Listen, if anything happens to me - and I mean anything - I need you to give the necklace to Evie. She'll keep it safe."

Albert's eyebrows shot up. "Evie? Are you sure that's wise, James? The less she knows, the safer she'll be."

James shook his head. "She's stronger than you think, and she deserves to know the truth. I'll leave clues in my journal, help guide her if the worst should happen."

He reached into his coat pocket and pulled out a small leather-bound book. "I've been keeping track of everything, Albert. The necklace, Sterling, the Task Force - it's all in here. If Evie ever needs to understand, this journal should help her piece it all together."

Albert took the journal, turning it over in his hands. "And where will you keep this?"

"There's a hidden spot in the Hawthorn Manor library," James replied. "Hidden, but not impossible to find if someone's looking. I'll make sure Evie knows where it's location if she ever needs it. That library holds more secrets than anyone, including Evie, knows."

Albert nodded, a mix of admiration and concern in his eyes. "You've thought this through, haven't you?"

James offered a grim smile. "I have to. We're in deep, Albert, and I need to make sure the truth comes out, with or without me."

One month passed, and life at Hawthorn Manor settled into a deceptive calm. James Grant maintained his routine, tending to the estate and occasionally visiting community events. The weight of their secret lingered, but outwardly, all seemed normal.

On a crisp Saturday morning in October, James set out for his usual walk in the city lake park. The leaves had begun to turn, painting the landscape in vibrant hues of red and gold. He strolled along the familiar paths, nodding to fellow regulars and pausing to admire the autumn foliage reflected in the still waters of the lake.

Later that morning, a jogger stumbled upon James's body near a secluded bench overlooking the water. Despite the paramedics' best efforts, James Grant was pronounced dead at the scene. The official cause of death was listed as a heart attack, a seemingly natural end for a man of his age.

News of James' passing spread quickly through the town. Evelyn was devastated, retreating into the quiet halls of Hawthorn Manor to grieve. Albert closed his shop for a month, unable to face customers while mourning his old friend.

But as the initial shock subsided, whispers began to circulate in the art world. Art dealers huddled over coffee, their voices low as they shared their suspicions. In the aisles of the galleries, people exchanged meaningful glances and hushed theories.

"It just doesn't sit right," Mrs. Thompson murmured to her husband. "James was as healthy as a horse. A heart attack?"

The rumors gained traction when someone recalled seeing a sleek black car parked near the lake on the day of James's death. Another claimed to have spotted a man in a dark suit lurking near the park entrance.

Sterling's name began to surface in these hushed conversations with increasing frequency. His long-standing rivalry with James was no secret in the art world. Sterling ran James down in social circles, spreading thinly veiled accusations about fraudulent dealings and questionable wartime activities, while James maintained a dignified silence. The two were never seen in the same room, and art gallery openings were carefully orchestrated to ensure their paths wouldn't cross. Even mutual acquaintances learned to host separate events, knowing that inviting both men would lead to uncomfortable tensions and whispered gossip among the guests. Many people already harbored deep suspicions about the Sterling Galleria's ties to organized crime or the Russian mafia. Whispers of clandestine meetings and shadowy deals swirled around the Sterling's pristine gallery, casting a pall over its gleaming facade.

James Grant, on the other hand, had been a well-known art collector and wealthy pillar of the community. His personal collection was rumored to be worth hundreds of millions, a treasure trove of rare and coveted pieces that spanned centuries and continents. However, James wasn't entirely absolved from the rumors that he himself had dabbled in selling onto the black market. Some speculated that his own hands weren't entirely clean, adding another layer of intrigue to his sudden demise. The community as a whole took keen note of his death, with many wondering what secrets might have died with him and what treasures might now be up for grabs in the cutthroat world of high-stakes art collecting.

As the days passed, the official story of a heart attack began to feel increasingly hollow among those who knew James best. The seeds of doubt had been planted, and in the fertile soil of city gossip, they quickly took root.

In the weeks following James's funeral, Evelyn Grant found herself adrift in a sea of grief. The halls of Hawthorn Manor echoed with memories of her late husband, each room a reminder of their shared life and secrets. She spent her days wandering from room to room, touching familiar objects and struggling to come to terms with her new reality.

As executor of James's estate, Evelyn was overwhelmed by the complexities of managing their extensive art collection. Paperwork piled up on James's old desk, and inquiries from auction houses and galleries went unanswered. The weight of responsibility pressed down on her, threatening to crush her spirit entirely.

It was Albert who first reached out, gently knocking on the manor's heavy oak door one crisp autumn morning. Evelyn answered, her eyes red-rimmed and distant.

"Evie," Albert said softly, removing his flat cap. "I thought you might need a friend."

Evelyn nodded, stepping aside to let him in. They sat in the study, surrounded by priceless paintings and antiques, sipping tea in silence. Finally, Albert spoke.

"James entrusted me with some of his affairs," he said carefully. "I'd like to help you navigate this, if you'll let me."

Evelyn's hands trembled as she set down her teacup. "I don't know where to begin, Albert. There's so much... so many questions."

Albert leaned forward, his green eyes kind but sharp. "We'll take it one step at a time. First, let's go through the immediate concerns with the collection."

Over the following weeks, Albert became a constant presence at Hawthorn Manor. He guided Evelyn through the intricacies of appraisals, insurance policies, and gallery contracts. His expertise in the art world proved invaluable as they sorted through James' extensive records and correspondence.

Evelyn found comfort in Albert's steady presence and dry humor. As they worked, she began to share stories of her life with James, the adventures they'd had, and the secrets they'd kept. Evelyn found herself reminiscing about how James, despite being twenty years her senior, had managed to sweep her off her feet with his charm and worldly wisdom. His silver-streaked hair and laugh lines had only added to his allure, and she remembered how his stories of far-off places and hidden treasures had captivated her young heart. The age difference, which might have given others pause, had seemed inconsequential in the face of their shared passion for art and history. James's gentle demeanor and quick wit had made her feel both protected and challenged, a combination that had proven irresistible to her younger self. Albert listened patiently, offering a sympathetic ear and, occasionally, insights that hinted at a deeper understanding of James's world than Evelyn had realized.

As Albert spent more time at Hawthorn Manor, helping Evelyn sort through James's affairs, it became increasingly clear that James had not shared all of his stories with his young wife. Albert noticed gaps in Evelyn's knowledge about certain pieces in the collection, particularly those acquired during James's time in Europe during and after the war.

One afternoon, while reviewing a ledger of acquisitions from the 1950s, Albert paused, his brow furrowing. He glanced at Evelyn, who was arranging papers on James's old desk.

"Evie," he said carefully, "did James ever mention a collection of Russian icons he acquired in '53?"

Evelyn looked up, puzzled. "Russian icons? No, I don't recall anything like that."

Albert nodded slowly, his suspicions confirmed. He realized that James had compartmentalized certain aspects of his life, keeping them separate from his relationship with Evelyn. It wasn't out of malice or distrust,

Albert knew, but rather a misguided attempt to protect her from the complexities and potential dangers of his past.

As they continued their work, more such instances came to light. References to meetings with mysterious collectors, cryptic notes about valuations that didn't match official records, and coded messages that hinted at transactions far more complex than simple art deals.

Albert began to understand that James had likely thought he had more time. The sudden nature of his death meant that he hadn't left behind the kind of detailed information that would have helped Evelyn navigate this hidden world. James had probably intended to share these secrets with her eventually, but fate had intervened before he could do so.

As the afternoon light began to fade, forming shadows across the study's walls, Albert reached into his tweed jacket pocket. He pulled out a small wooden box and a heavy envelope, its edges slightly worn. For a moment, he held it in his hand, his expression unreadable.

Evelyn looked up from the stack of papers she had been sorting, her eyes questioning. "What's that, Albert?"

Albert took a deep breath, his fingers tightening around the box. "Evie, there's something James entrusted to me. Something he wanted you to have when the time was right."

He crossed the room and gently placed the box and envelope in Evelyn's hands. She felt its weight, surprisingly heavy for its size. With curious fingers, she opened the lid and stared in disbelieve at the sight.

The Amara Necklace, a masterpiece in its own right. The sapphire at its center caught the fading light, sending blue fire dancing across the room. Evelyn gasped, her free hand flying to her mouth.

"Oh, Albert," she whispered, her eyes wide with shock and recognition. "Is this...?"

Albert nodded solemnly. "Yes, Evie. It's the Amara Necklace. James asked me to keep it safe and to give it to you when... well, when the time came."

Evelyn's fingers traced the intricate lace work of the chain, her touch reverent. Memories flooded back - hushed conversations between James and Albert, cryptic references to a precious object, the weight of unspoken secrets that had sometimes hung in the air.

"I don't understand," Evelyn said, her voice barely above a whisper. "Why didn't James tell me about this? Why keep it hidden?"

Albert sank into the chair across from her, his expression grave. "James wanted to protect you, Evie. He knew the necklace carried a history - and dangers - that he didn't want to burden you with."

For several hours, Albert shared half of what James had confided in him. The history of the necklace, its mystery, and its connection to the war. His voice growing hoarse as he delved into the intricate history. His eyes gleamed with a mixture of excitement and trepidation as he recounted tales of secret missions and clandestine exchanges. Albert also explained the complex relationship between James and Nikolai, painting a vivid picture of two men bound by duty yet divided by loyalty. He described their initial camaraderie, forged in the crucible of war, and the gradual erosion of trust as their interests diverged. The struggle between them, Albert revealed, was not just personal but emblematic of the larger conflict brewing between East and West. As he spoke, the weight of unspoken secrets and questions hung heavy in the air, hinting at even darker truths and answers that even Albert didn't know fully.

Chapter Fourteen

Cat and Maya stood before the imposing facade of Sterling Galleria, its ornate bronze doors gleaming in the afternoon sun. The cobblestone street bustled with well-heeled patrons and sleek luxury cars. Cat took a deep breath, steeling herself for what lay ahead.

"Ready?" Maya whispered, giving Cat's hand a reassuring squeeze.

Cat nodded, and they pushed through the heavy doors into a world of luxury and intrigue. The grand foyer took their breath away - marble floors, gilded moldings, and a chandelier that sparkled like a thousand stars. Well-dressed patrons milled about, their hushed conversations creating a soft murmur that filled the space.

As they moved deeper into the gallery, Maya's eyes darted from one priceless piece to another. Paintings that probably cost more than her family's entire home hung on pristine white walls. Sculptures stood proudly on pedestals, their curves and angles telling silent stories.

Maya leaned in close. "This place screams money. You sure we're not out of our league here?"

Cat shook her head, her determination evident in her eyes. "We have to be careful, but we can't back down now. Remember, we're looking for any connection to 1963 or my family."

They meandered through the main exhibition hall, trying to blend in with the crowd. Cat overheard snippets of conversation - talk of upcoming auctions, rare finds, and the ever-fluctuating art market. But beneath the polished veneer, she sensed an undercurrent of something darker.

As they rounded a corner, Cat froze. A glass case stood before them, housing a collection of antique jewelry. And there, nestled among the glittering gems, was a necklace that bore a resemblance to the one from her grandmother's attic.

"Maya," Cat whispered, her voice barely audible. "Look."

Maya's eyes widened as she followed Cat's gaze. "That looks like...?"

Before Cat could respond, a smooth, cultured voice spoke with a slight Russian accent from behind them. "Admiring our fine collection?"

The girls turned to find themselves face to face with a tall, impeccably dressed man with silver hair and piercing gray eyes. His smile was charming, but it didn't quite reach his eyes.

"Viktor Sterling," he introduced himself, extending a hand. "Welcome to my gallery."

Cat's heart raced as she shook Viktor Sterling's hand, acutely aware of the power this man wielded in the art world. His grip was firm, his smile practiced and polite. Maya stood slightly behind Cat, her usual Type A personality tempered by the gravity of the moment.

"It's a pleasure to meet you, Mr. Sterling," Cat said, her voice steadier than she felt. "Your gallery is truly impressive."

Viktor's eyes sparkled with pride. "Thank you, my dear. My father spent decades curating only the finest pieces. Sadly, he passed some time ago, leaving this legacy to me. Are you an art enthusiast yourself?"

Cat nodded, thinking quickly. "I'm fascinated by the stories behind each piece. The history, the journey they've taken to end up here."

"Ah, a girl after my own heart," Viktor chuckled. He gestured to the case before them. "These jewels, for instance, each have a tale to tell. Do any catch your eye?"

Cat's gaze lingered on the necklace that resembled her grandmother's. "They're all beautiful, but I'm particularly drawn to antique pieces."

Viktor raised an eyebrow, his interest piqued. "Oh? And why is that?"

"I suppose it's the mystery," Cat replied, choosing her words carefully. "You never know what secrets they might hold."

Viktor's smile widened, but there was a calculating look in his eyes. "Indeed. One must be careful, though. Some secrets are best untold."

Cat took a deep breath, sensing an opening. It was now or never. "Actually, Mr. Sterling, I was wondering if you could tell me anything about a particular piece.

Have you ever come across something called the Amara Necklace?"

The effect was instantaneous. Viktor's carefully crafted facade cracked, his eyes widening in shock. The color drained from his face, and for a moment, he seemed at a loss for words. His hand, which had been gesturing casually, froze in mid-air.

"The... Amara Necklace?" he repeated, his voice suddenly hoarse. "Where... where did you hear that name?"

Viktor's composure returned quickly, but his eyes remained fixed on Cat with newfound intensity. He glanced around the gallery, ensuring no one was within earshot, before leaning in closer.

"My dear, you've stumbled upon quite a sensitive topic," Viktor said, his voice low and measured. "The Amara Necklace is not something one discusses lightly in these circles."

Cat's heart raced, but she held Viktor's gaze steadily. "Why is that, Mr. Sterling?"

Viktor sighed, running a hand through his silver hair. "Because, young lady, the Amara Necklace has been missing from antiquity for many years. No one knows the current owner. No one knows where it is. It wasn't just a single piece, but part of a larger collection—priceless artifacts and jewels, each with its own storied past. Many of which were stolen from this very Galleria in 1963. It had belonged to my father, but was stolen by an unknown person."

Maya shifted uncomfortably beside Cat, but remained silent, her eyes darting between her friend and the imposing gallery owner.

"The collection was stolen?" Cat pressed, trying to keep her voice neutral.

Viktor nodded, a hint of admiration creeping into his expression. "Indeed. Well, not the entire collection. We have a few of the seven pieces in our possession. Several others were taken along with a treasure trove of collectables from the private vault in the heist. The entire art world was in an uproar. Some pieces have been rescued over the years, but many, including the Amara Necklace, remain lost."

Cat's mind whirled, connecting this new information to the clues she'd uncovered. The date matched the entry in her grandfather's journal.

"What makes the Amara Necklace so special?" she asked, careful not to reveal too much of her own knowledge.

Viktor's eyes gleamed. "Oh, it's not just about the exquisite craftsmanship or the rare blue sapphire. The Amara Necklace is said to hold secrets—a key to something far more valuable than mere jewels. Its worth goes beyond anything you could imagine."

Cat felt the atmosphere shift as Viktor's piercing gaze bore into her. His initial shock had given way to a calculated wariness, and she sensed his growing suspicion with each passing moment. The surrounding air seemed to thicken, charged with unspoken questions and hidden agendas.

"I'm curious," Viktor said, his voice low and measured. "What sparked your interest in such a specific piece? The Amara Necklace isn't exactly common knowledge, especially among... younger enthusiasts."

Cat's mind raced, searching for a plausible explanation. "I came across it in an old art history book," she lied smoothly, hoping her face didn't betray her nerves. "The story fascinated me, and I've been researching it ever since."

Viktor's eyes narrowed slightly, a ghost of a smile playing on his lips. "Is that so? Well, you've certainly stumbled upon one of the art world's greatest mysteries."

He glanced around the gallery once more before continuing, his voice barely above a whisper. "The theft of the Amara Necklace remains one of the most baffling unsolved cases in modern art history. Decades have passed, and yet no one has been able to trace its whereabouts or the identify the culprits."

Cat's heart raced as she absorbed this information. The urgency of her investigation suddenly felt more pressing than ever.

"Has there been any progress in the case recently?" she asked, trying to keep her tone casual.

Viktor's expression darkened. "There are always rumors, whispers of who has it, roamers of where it might be. But nothing concrete. The necklace, along with the other priceless pieces from that collection, seems to have vanished into thin air."

He leaned in closer, his voice taking on a conspiratorial tone. "Some say the necklace is cursed, bringing misfortune to anyone who possesses it. Others believe it holds the key to an even greater treasure. But one thing is certain—I would stop at nothing to get it back... for the Galleria, of course."

Cat's heart pounded as she processed Viktor's words. The gravity of the situation settled over her like a heavy cloak, but instead of fear, she felt a surge of determination. This wasn't just about satisfying her curiosity anymore; it was about uncovering a truth that had been buried for decades, a truth that was intimately connected to her family.

She glanced at Maya, who gave her a subtle nod of encouragement. Cat took a deep breath, steeling herself for what lay ahead. The warnings, the secrecy, the potential danger—none of it mattered now. She had come too far to turn back.

"Thank you for sharing this information, Mr. Sterling," Cat said, her voice steady despite the turmoil inside her. "It's fascinating to hear about the necklace's history from someone so knowledgeable."

Viktor studied her face intently, his piercing gaze searching for any hint of deception. "You're quite welcome, my dear. But I must caution you—curiosity about such matters can be... dangerous. There are those who would betray their own families to keep the necklace hidden."

Cat nodded, her mind racing. She stood at a crossroads, faced with a crucial decision. Should she confide in Viktor, revealing what she knew about the necklace?

Or should she guard her knowledge, keeping her cards close to her chest?

She looked up at Viktor, taking in his calculating expression and the glint in his eyes. Despite his charm and apparent openness, something about him set her on edge. Her instincts screamed at her to be cautious.

"I appreciate your concern, Mr. Sterling," Cat said finally, choosing her words with care. "Rest assured, my interest is purely academic. I wouldn't want to get involved in anything... complicated."

Viktor Sterling stood up straight, giving Cat and Maya a half hearted fake smile, turned on his heels and casually walked away. Cat and Maya studied him as he took his cell phone out of his expensive suit pocket and dialed a number while we walked away.

Chapter Fifteen

The tension in the Sterling Galleria hung thick in the air as Cat and Maya moved through the lavish space. Their footsteps echoed softly on the polished marble floors, each step carrying the weight of their newfound knowledge. Cat's mind raced, piecing together the fragments of information she'd gathered about the Amara Necklace.

Viktor's words summarized in her ears: 'There are powerful people out there who would stop at nothing to get their hands on it.' She glanced over her shoulder, half-expecting to see shadowy figures lurking behind the priceless artworks.

Maya leaned in close, her voice barely above a whisper. "Cat, this is getting intense. Maybe we should bail?"

Cat shook her head, her eyes scanning the room. "We can't leave now. That would look very suspicious."

They paused before a display case housing an array of antique jewelry. Cat's breath caught in her throat as she spotted another pendant that bore a striking resemblance to the one in her grandfather's journal. The sapphire with the snake entwined around it gleamed under the gallery lights, its deep blue hue seeming to hold secrets of its own.

"Look," Cat murmured, pointing discreetly. "Another necklace. That design... it's very similar to the other necklace."

Maya's eyes widened. "Holy crap, you're right. But how-"

A voice behind them made them both jump. "Admiring our exquisite collection?"

They turned to find a mid-aged gallery assistant, her smile polite but her eyes sharp and assessing. Cat forced a casual nod, acutely aware of how out of place they must look among the well-to-do patrons.

"It's beautiful," Cat managed, her heart pounding. "The craftsmanship is incredible."

The assistant launched into a detailed explanation of the piece's history, but Cat barely heard her. Her mind was racing, connecting dots and forming theories. The necklace's presence here couldn't be a coincidence. Was there more of a connection between the Sterling Galleria the Amara Necklace's than Viktor had let on? How did it end up in the attic?

As they moved away from the display, Cat felt the weight of unseen eyes upon them. The gallery's elegant facade suddenly seemed sinister, its beauty a mask for darker secrets. Every patron, every staff member became a potential enemy or ally in a game Cat was only beginning to understand. At this point, she had to treat everyone as a threat until she understood more.

Cat's gaze swept across the gallery, taking in the meticulously arranged artwork and the patrons admiring them. As she turned her head, a flicker of movement caught her eye. In the shadows near a dimly lit alcove, a figure stood motionless, partially obscured by a large sculpture.

She blinked, shaking her head slightly. The gallery's lighting played tricks, casting strange shadows and reflections. Cat tried to focus on the conversation with Maya, but her eyes kept drifting back to that spot.

"You okay?" Maya asked, noticing her distraction.

"Yeah, just thought I saw..." Cat trailed off, realizing the figure was gone. "Never mind. This place is giving me the creeps."

They continued their tour, but Cat couldn't shake the feeling of unease that settled over her. The hairs on the back of her neck stood up, and she found herself glancing over her shoulder more frequently.

As they paused before an abstract painting, Cat caught another glimpse of movement in her peripheral vision. This time, she was certain - a tall, dark-clad figure ducked behind a pillar, clearly trying to avoid being seen.

Cat's heart rate quickened. She grabbed Maya's arm, pulling her closer.

"Don't look now, but I think someone's watching us," she whispered.

Maya's eyes widened, but she managed to keep her voice low. "Are you sure?"

Cat nodded, her eyes darting around the room. "By the sculpture garden. I've seen them twice now."

They pretended to admire a nearby painting, but Cat's senses were on high alert. The gallery suddenly felt claustrophobic, its elegant rooms transformed into a maze of potential dangers. Every shadow seemed to conceal a threat, every murmured conversation a possible plot against them.

As they moved to another exhibit, Cat caught sight of the figure again. This time, there was no mistaking the intent - whoever it was, they were definitely following her and Maya through the gallery.

Cat's heart raced as she watched the mysterious figure weave through the gallery, drawing ever closer. She gripped Maya's arm, her voice barely above a whisper. "We need to move. Now."

Maya nodded, her eyes wide with concern. They quickened their pace, ducking behind a large abstract sculpture. Cat's mind whirred, searching for an escape route.

The large figure emerged from behind a pillar. He moved with purpose, his gaze fixed on Cat's last known position. As he drew near, Cat caught a glimpse of him - black suit, muscular build, chiseled face, with cold black eyes that scanned the room quickly and methodically.

"There's something off about him," Cat murmured to Maya. "He doesn't look like his here to admire the art. We need to get out of here."

They edged towards the main hall, trying to blend in with a group of art enthusiasts. But the man was relentless, cutting through the crowd with practiced ease. Cat felt the panic rising in her chest as she realized he was herding them towards a quieter corner of the gallery.

Just as it seemed he would corner them, Cat's eyes landed on a "Staff Only" door tucked away behind a velvet rope. Without hesitation, she grabbed Maya's hand and made a beeline for it.

"Cat, what are you-" Maya started, but Cat was already ducking under the rope.

"Trust me," Cat snapped, her hand on the door handle. She glanced back, seeing the man quicken his pace, his hand reaching into his jacket.

Cat pushed the door open, pulling Maya through with her. They found themselves in a narrow hallway lined with storage crates and framed artwork waiting to be hung.

"Quick, help me with this," Cat said, grabbing a large empty crate. Together, they dragged it in front of the door just as they heard footsteps approaching from the other side.

Cat's mind raced as she scanned the narrow hallway, searching for an escape route. The sound of the door handle rattling behind them sent a jolt of adrenaline through her body. She knew they had only moments before their pursuer broke through.

"This way," Cat whispered urgently, pulling Maya towards a bend in the corridor. As they rounded the corner, they found themselves in a larger storage area filled with crates and partially unwrapped sculptures.

The sound of splintering wood echoed through the hallway. Their makeshift barricade had failed.

Cat's eyes darted around the room, landing on a stack of empty frames leaning against the wall. A plan formed in her mind.

"Maya, when I say go, run for that door," Cat instructed, pointing to an exit sign at the far end of the room. "Don't stop, no matter what."

Maya nodded, her face pale but determined.

Cat took a deep breath, steadying herself. As the footsteps grew closer, she positioned herself near the stack of frames.

The moment the figure appeared in the doorway, Cat sprung into action.

"Maya, now!" she shouted, shoving the stack of frames with all her might. The frames clattered to the floor with a deafening crash, creating a barrier between them and their pursuer.

In the chaos, Cat caught a glimpse of Maya darting towards the exit. The man stumbled, momentarily caught off guard by the falling debris.

Cat seized the opportunity, grabbing a small sculpture from a nearby crate and hurling it across the room. "Hey!" she yelled, drawing the man's attention away from Maya's retreating form.

The distraction worked. The figure's head snapped towards Cat, his cold eyes locking onto her. Cat's heart pounded as she realized she was now the sole focus of his pursuit.

Cat burst through the exit door, ironically, the very door her grandfather had snuck through all those years ago. Her heart pounding in her chest. She scanned the area frantically, relief washing over her as she spotted Maya waiting anxiously by a nearby alleyway.

"Maya!" Cat gasped, rushing over to her friend. "Thank God you're okay."

Maya's eyes widened as she took in Cat's disheveled appearance. "Cat, what happened in there? Who was that guy?"

Cat glanced over her shoulder, making sure they weren't followed. "I don't know, but he was definitely after us. We need to get out of here."

They hurried down the alley, putting distance between themselves and the gallery. Once they felt relatively safe, Cat leaned against a wall, trying to catch her breath.

"Okay, spill," Maya demanded. "What the hell is going on?"

Cat ran a hand through her hair, her mind racing. "That man, whoever he is, he's connected to all of this somehow. The necklace, the gallery, my family's secrets - it's all tied together."

Maya's expression shifted from confusion to determination. "Alright, we need a plan. What do we know so far?"

Cat took a deep breath, organizing her thoughts. "The Amara Necklace is more than just a secret family heirloom. It's connected to some kind of art heist back in

1963. And now, people are willing to chase us through an art gallery because we asked question about it."

Maya nodded, her brow furrowed in concentration. "So, what's our next move?"

"We need to dig deeper," Cat said, her resolve strengthening. "There's got to be more information out there about the heist. Maybe newspaper archives or old police reports?"

"I can help with that," Maya offered. "My aunt works at the city library on 4th street. She might be able to give us access to their archives."

Cat felt a surge of gratitude for her friend's unwavering support. "That's perfect. We should also try to find out more about Viktor Sterling and his connection to all of this."

As they discussed their next steps, Cat couldn't shake the feeling that they were in over their heads.

Chapter Sixteen

Cat and Maya approached the city library, a grand old building with stone columns and wide steps leading to its entrance. As they climbed the stairs, Maya nudged Cat.

"There's my Aunt Rosey," she whispered, pointing to a woman with graying hair tied back in a neat bun.

Rosey greeted them with a warm smile. "Maya, dear! And you must be Cat. What can I help you girls with today?"

Cat hesitated, unsure how much to reveal. Maya jumped in. "We're doing a research project on local history. We were hoping to access some old newspapers and records."

Rosey's eyes lit up. "Oh, how wonderful! I love seeing young people interested in history. Follow me, girls."

She led them through the library's main floor and down a narrow staircase. The air grew cooler and mustier as they descended.

"The archives are down here," Rosey explained, unlocking a heavy door. "It's not the most glamorous space, but it's a treasure trove of information."

Cat's eyes widened as they entered. The basement stretched out before them, filled with rows upon rows of filing cabinets and shelves stacked with boxes.

Rosey pointed to a desk near the entrance. "That's where you'll find the catalog. It'll help you locate specific records. If you need anything, just ring the bell on the desk, and someone will come down to assist you."

As Rosey turned to leave, Cat called out, "Actually, we're looking for information about an art heist in 1963. Do you know where we might start?"

Rosey paused, her brow furrowing. "1963, you say? Try the archives from that year. They're in the back left corner. Good luck with your research, girls!"

As Rosey's footsteps faded, Cat and Maya exchanged excited glances. They made their way through the dimly lit room, their footsteps echoing in the massive space.

"This place is creepy," Maya whispered, her voice hushed in the silence.

Cat nodded, feeling a mix of excitement and apprehension. As they neared the back of the room, Maya suddenly let out a loud sneeze, the sound reverberating off the walls.

A stern-faced archivist appeared from behind a nearby shelf, fixing them with a disapproving glare. Maya mouthed a silent "sorry" as Cat suppressed a nervous giggle.

Cat and Maya make their way to where Aunt Rosey had directed. The floor slick from built up dust. The files are meticulously arranged, and they easily found a label for 1963. Cat immediately looked for June 1963. After only a few moments, she arrived at the right box.

Cat's fingers trembled slightly as she carefully opened the lid. Inside the city labeled orange box was the newspaper of the day, and several documents, along with a police report. She scanned the police reports, her eyes widening as she took in the information.

"Maya," she whispered urgently, "look at this. I found a report on the heist."

Maya leaned in close, her breath warm on Cat's cheek as they both examined the paper.

"It's a list of items that were stolen," Cat explained, her voice barely above a whisper. "And look at the entry of one of the owners of an item that was stolen—it's linked to an antique shop owned by Albert Carlisle."

Maya's brow furrowed. "Albert Carlisle? Why does that name sound familiar?"

Cat's heart raced as she pointed to a few specific entries on the list. "These items... they were supposed to be auctioned off. And they belonged to him."

Their eyes met, a spark of excitement passing between them. Without a word, they both knew they'd stumbled upon something significant.

"This could be huge, Cat," Maya breathed, her voice tinged with awe. "We need to dig deeper into this Albert Carlisle guy."

Cat nodded, her mind already racing with possibilities. She carefully folded the document and slipped it into her bag, making sure to note its original location in the archives.

As they continued to sift through the old records, Cat couldn't shake the feeling that they were on the brink of uncovering something big. The connection between Albert Carlisle, the antique shop, and the stolen auctioned items seemed to be a crucial piece of the puzzle.

Maya's voice cut through her thoughts. "Hey Cat, I found something else. Look at this old newspaper clipping."

Cat leaned in, her heart pounding as she read the faded print. The article mentioned Albert Carlisle's antique shop and hinted of few high-profile sales running through the Sterling Galleria.

They exchanged meaningful glances, realizing they'd stumbled upon a potential goldmine of information. The pieces were starting to fall into place, and Cat could feel the excitement building in her chest.

"Next stop, Carlisle Antique Shop," Cat said sharply.

Cat and Maya approached the weathered storefront of Carlisle's Antiques. The shop window displayed an eclectic array of vintage items, from ornate silver candlesticks to faded leather-bound books. Cat's eyes darted across the display, searching for anything that might resemble the necklace or other artifacts from her grandmother's attic.

Maya nudged her friend's shoulder. "You ready for this?"

Cat hesitated, her hand hovering over the door handle. The peeling paint and slightly crooked sign gave the shop a shabby, forgotten air. She took a deep breath, readying herself for whatever they might discover inside.

"As ready as I'll ever be," Cat murmured.

With a determined push, she opened the door. A small bell jingled overhead, announcing their arrival. The sound echoed through the cluttered interior, bouncing off shelves crammed with curios and antiques.

The musty scent of old books and wood enveloped them as they stepped inside. Dust particles danced in the shafts of afternoon sunlight streaming through the grimy windows. Cat's eyes adjusted to the dim interior, taking in the cramped aisles and towering shelves.

Maya whispered, "Whoa, this place is like a time capsule."

Cat nodded, her gaze sweeping across the shop. Every surface seemed covered with some relic from the past - tarnished silverware, delicate porcelain figurines, and faded photographs in ornate frames. The sheer volume of items was overwhelming, but Cat forced herself to focus.

They made their way deeper into the shop, careful not to bump into the overly stacked piles of books and boxes. Cat's heart raced as she scanned for anything that might connect to her family's mystery.

As Cat and Maya ventured deeper into the cluttered shop, an elderly man emerged from behind a towering stack of books. His wispy gray hair peeked out from beneath a well-worn flat cap, and he peered at them over wire-rimmed spectacles.

"Can I help you girls?" he asked, his voice gravelly but not unkind.

Cat stepped forward, her heart pounding. "We're looking for information about an antique necklace. The Amara Necklace?"

The old man's eyes narrowed slightly, a flicker of recognition passing across his weathered face. "Ah, the Amara Necklace. That's quite a specific inquiry. What's your interest in it?"

As he spoke, Cat felt a jolt of familiarity. The cadence of his voice, the slight rasp—it tugged at her memory.

"It's for a school project," Maya chimed in smoothly, covering for Cat's hesitation.

The man nodded slowly, his eyes twinkling with a hint of intrigue. "Well, the Amara Necklace is believed to be quite the artifact, my dears. It's said to have belonged to European royalty before vanishing mysteriously in the 19th century. Some even claim it holds mystical properties, though that's likely just fanciful speculation," he said as he held his hands up wiggling his fingers mystically.

He turned, using his cane to move towards a nearby bookshelf lined with ancient books and weathered volumes. "Let me see if I can find a reference book for you. I believe I have just the thing that might shed some light on this enigmatic piece."

Cat's eyes widened as she watched him walk, her heart quickening. The stutter in his step, the way he used his cane—it was unmistakable and eerily familiar.

Was this possibly the man she'd overheard talking to her grandmother in the library that day? The pieces of the puzzle were slowly falling into place. But the connections were eluding her.

As he returned with a dusty book, its leather binding cracked with age, Cat's mind raced with possibilities. Who was this man, really, and how was he connected to her family's long-buried secrets? What role did he play in the mystery surrounding the necklace?

"Here we are," he said, placing the book on the counter with a gentle thud. "This might give you some background on the necklace's history. It's quite a fascinating tale, full of intrigue and unanswered questions."

Cat nodded, struggling to keep her voice steady as she fought to contain her excitement and suspicion. "Thank you, Mr...?" she trailed off, fishing for more information.

"Carlisle," he replied, a ghost of a smile playing on his lips. "Albert Carlisle. But you can call me Bertie if you'd like.

Cat's heart raced as she gathered her courage. "Mr. Carlisle, what can you tell us about Viktor Sterling and the heist at his gallery in 1963?"

Albert's eyes narrowed, his demeanor shifting from genial to guarded in an instant. He glanced around the shop, as if checking for eavesdroppers, before leaning in closer.

"Now that's an event I haven't thought of in a long time," he said, his voice low and gravelly. "Viktor Sterling is not someone to be trifled with, my dear. He's a dangerous man, with fingers in many pies—some less savory than others. His father, Nikolai Sterling, founded the Galleria in the 1950s. Their Russian if you couldn't tell by the name. Viktor took over the family business after Nikolai died. Rumor has it the Sterlings were tied into the KGB or the Russian mob. Lots of people looked into it, none could ever prove anything."

Cat and Maya exchanged worried glances as Bertie continued.

"The heist in '63 was a messy business. I lost several pieces in that heist. pieces I had held for a long time. Valuable pieces disappeared overnight, including some items with... shall we say, questionable provenance? Ol' Nikolai was furious, but there were whispers that he might have orchestrated it himself for the insurance money. He stood to make a fortune either way, in my opinion."

Albert's eyes locked onto Cat's, his gaze intense. "But let me tell you something, girl. If Sterling is sniffing around for that necklace you're asking about, you'd best steer clear. He'd do anything to get his hands on it—and I mean anything."

The old man's words sent a chill down Cat's spine. She swallowed hard, trying to keep her voice steady. "Why is he so interested in the Amara Necklace?"

Albert shook his head, a wry smile on his weathered face. "That necklace isn't just a pretty trinket. It's a key to something far greater. His father was after it, and now Viktor is carrying on the family tradition, I suppose. They have been chasing it for decades, and they're not the type to give up easily."

Albert's eyes darted around the shop once more before he leaned in, his voice dropping to a conspiratorial whisper. "There's a story that's been circulating in certain circles for decades. It's not the kind of tale you'll find in history books, mind you."

Cat and Maya exchanged glances, their curiosity piqued.

"After the war ended, there was chaos everywhere, especially in Germany. The Nazis had looted countless treasures from all over Europe, and in the aftermath, some of those artifacts... well, they didn't exactly make it back to their rightful owners."

He paused, running a gnarled hand through his wispy hair. "You see, there were those who saw an opportunity in the confusion. Some Allied soldiers, Soviet soldiers, art experts, even government officials—they took it upon themselves to 'protect' certain valuable pieces."

Cat's brow furrowed. "You mean they stole them?"

Albert shrugged. "That's a matter of perspective, I suppose. They'd argue they were safeguarding these treasures from falling into the wrong hands. The Soviets were advancing, and there was fear that priceless artifacts might disappear behind the Iron Curtain."

Maya leaned forward, captivated. "So what happened to these so called 'artifacts'?" She said as she used air quotes around the word 'artifacts'.

"Many of them vanished into private collections," Albert continued. "Wealthy collectors, secret vaults, hidden away from the public eye. Some say these pieces are still out there, passed down through families or traded in underground markets."

He fixed his gaze on Cat. "The Amara Necklace... well, it's not hard to imagine it might have been caught up in such affairs. A piece like that, with its history and supposed mystical properties, would have been quite the prize."

Cat's mind raced, connecting the dots between Albert's tale and her family's secrets. "And you think Viktor Sterling is after these smuggled artifacts?"

Albert nodded gravely. "The Sterling's made it their life's work to track down these lost treasures. He's not just after the prestige—he's obsessed with the power they represent."

Albert's gaze softened as he looked at Cat. "I knew your grandfather, James Grant. We had some dealings over the years."

Cat's eyes widened. "You did? What was he like?"

The old man chuckled, a fond expression crossing his weathered face. "Grant was a private man, that's for certain. He always seemed to know more than he let on. Had a keen eye for valuable pieces, too."

Maya nudged Cat with her elbow, sensing the importance of this revelation.

Albert continued, his voice taking on a thoughtful tone. "Your grandfather... he had a way about him. Could walk into a room full of artifacts and pick out the most valuable piece without hesitation. It was like he had a sixth sense for it."

Cat leaned in, hanging on every word. "Did he ever mention anything about the Amara Necklace to you?"

The shopkeeper shook his head. "Not directly, no. But there was something interesting he did mention once." He paused, his brow furrowing as if recalling a distant memory. "Grant told me he knew Viktor Sterling's father from the war."

"Viktor Sterling's father?" Cat repeated, surprise evident in her voice.

Albert nodded. "Yes, said they were both involved in recovering stolen art. Found that quite intriguing, I did. Makes you wonder about the connections, doesn't it?"

Cat's mind raced, piecing together this new information. Her grandfather had known Viktor Sterling's father during the war, both of them working to recover stolen art. And now, decades later, Viktor was pursuing the very necklace that had somehow ended up in her family's possession.

"Did my grandfather ever say anything else about Viktor's father?" Cat pressed, hoping for more details.

Albert shook his head. "I'm afraid not. Like I said, James was a private man. But the way he spoke about it... there was a lot of tension there."

Albert leaned forward and stared directly into Cat's eyes, his voice barely above a whisper. "Listen carefully. If you know where that necklace is, keep it hidden and don't talk about it. Viktor won't hesitate to use whatever means necessary to get what he wants. He's got connections in low places and isn't afraid to use them. If he even thinks you have it, you'll be in grave danger."

The weight of the revelations made Cat's stomach drop and feel a little nauseated. She knew the risks had just doubled. Cat and Maya thanked Albert for his time and made their exit.

Cat and Maya exited Carlisle's Antiques, the bell above the door chiming softly as they stepped onto the sun-drenched sidewalk. The afternoon heat enveloped them, a stark contrast to the cool but damp interior of the shop they'd just left. The air shimmered with the intensity of the summer day, making the bustling street before them seem almost surreal.

As they walked towards Maya's car, Cat's brow furrowed deeply, her mind churning with unanswered questions. She glanced back at the weathered storefront, its windows filled with an eclectic array of curiosities, then turned to her friend, her eyes alight with suspicion.

"Maya, did you notice something odd?" Cat asked, her voice low and tinged with concern.

Maya raised an eyebrow, a hint of amusement playing across her features. "You mean besides the creepy old shop full of dusty antiques and cryptic warnings? I swear I saw a shrunken head in there."

Cat shook her head emphatically, her ponytail swishing with the motion. "No, I mean about Mr. Carlisle. He knew who I was, but I never told him my name... yet he knew exactly who I was."

Maya's eyes widened as realization dawned on her face, her usual carefree expression replaced by one of surprise and intrigue. "You're right. He just started talking about your grandfather like he already knew exactly who you were. That's... unsettling."

Cat nodded, her suspicions confirmed by her friend's reaction. "And remember that guy I heard in the library with my grandmother? The one with the gravelly voice?"

"Yeah, what about him?" Maya asked, her curiosity piqued.

"I think it was Mr. Carlisle," Cat replied, her voice barely above a whisper. "The voice, the way he walked—it all fits."

Maya let out a low whistle, running a hand through her hair. "Whoa. That's some serious spy movie stuff right there. But why would he be talking to your grandma right after you found the necklace? It can't be a coincidence."

Cat shrugged, her mind racing with possibilities, each more intriguing than the last. "I think my grandmother got spooked when I found it and started asking questions. She must have called him for advice or something. Which means they know each other pretty well. Maybe even better than we think."

They reached Maya's car, a beat-up sedan that had seen better days, and climbed in. The car air conditioning offered a brief respite from the oppressive heat outside, and both girls sighed in relief as they settled into their seats.

"So, what do we do now?" Maya asked, her hands resting on the steering wheel, fingers tapping out a nervous rhythm. "You're not going to let this go, are you?"

Cat stared out the windshield, her expression set in determination. The bustling street before them seemed to fade away as she focused on their next move. "We keep digging. Mr. Carlisle gave us some valuable information, even if it wasn't the full story. We need to find out more about my grandfather's connection to Viktor Sterling's father and what really happened during the war. There's something big here, Maya. I can feel it."

Chapter Seventeen

Later that evening, Viktor Sterling leaned back in his sleek leather chair, his cold gray eyes fixed on the array of jewels spread across his glass desk as he sipped a short glass of imported vodka. His attempt to have his henchman apprehend the girls had failed. He almost regretted the extent he'd undergone to collect art over the years, but it had all been worth the risk so far.

He sat staring at six exquisite necklaces glittering under the office's soft overhead lighting, their beauty marred only by the conspicuous absence at their center. Viktor's jaw clenched as he contemplated the missing piece - the Amara Necklace.

His manicured fingers brushed over the faded papers scattered beside the jewels. His father's letters, each one a testament to a decades-old betrayal. Viktor's gaze lingered on a particular letter dated 1947. One name stood out, circled in faded red ink and written in all caps: JAMES GRANT.

Viktor's lips curled into a sneer as he read the passage again. His father's words burned with anger and accusation, detailing how the necklace had been stolen from him. The name of Grant was mentioned repeatedly, always in connection with the necklace.

Over the course of his childhood, his father Nikolai had talked about the Grants with such venomous disgust that it bordered on obsession. The hatred had been methodically ingrained into Viktor from an early age, a constant drumbeat of accusations and dark mutterings about how the Grants were duplicitous snakes who couldn't be trusted. Though Viktor would later discover that most of the stories his father told about James Grant were either grossly exaggerated or flat-out lies, crafted to feed a decades-old vendetta. As Viktor became of age, the talk from his senior-aged father about James Grant seemed to gradually die down, replaced by an almost manic fixation on the Amara necklace that consumed him until the day he died from cirrhosis of the liver - a familiar ending for most men in the Sterling line, who found solace at the bottom of expensive crystal decanters.

Now that Viktor had taken over the family business as Nikolai's only son and heir, he was determined to finish what his father had started, to complete the collection that had become his inheritance and his burden. It had taken considerable time, resources, and millions in carefully concealed payments to ensure six of the seven necklaces were secured in his private vault. The only piece missing was the centerpiece, the crown jewel of the collection. It wasn't lost on Viktor that the Grant family either had possession of the necklace or, at the minimum, knew of its whereabouts - a fact that made the pursuit all the more personal, all the more satisfying to contemplate.

He picked up one of the jewels, turning it over in his hand. The piece was exquisite, a marvel of craftsmanship that spoke of a bygone era. But without the Amara Necklace, it was incomplete. The collection - his father's legacy - remained unfinished.

Viktor set the jewels down with careful precision. His eyes darted to a framed photograph on his desk, showing a much younger version of himself standing beside his father. The elder Sterling's face was stern, his eyes holding the same cold determination that now resided in Viktor's gaze.

"I'll finish what you started, Father. That girl knows something," Viktor murmured in Russian, his voice barely above a whisper in the silent office. He turned back to the letters, his fingers tracing the circled name 'James Grant'. The men who he felt wronged his family, who had stolen what rightfully belonged to the Sterlings.

Chapter Eighteen

Cat returned to Hawthorn Manor as the sun dipped below the horizon, casting long shadows across the sprawling estate. The Victorian Gothic mansion loomed before her, its dark red brickwork and ivy-covered walls holding secrets she was only beginning to unravel. The old oak trees that lined the driveway seemed to whisper ancient tales as a cool breeze rustled through their leaves.

Inside, she found Evelyn in the library, seated in her favorite armchair by the fireplace. The older woman looked up as Cat entered, her blue eyes sharp despite her age. The room was bathed in a warm, golden glow from the antique lamps, and the scent of old books and polished wood hung in the air.

"Grandma, we need to talk," Cat said, her voice firm but gentle. She couldn't help but notice the slight tremor in her grandmother's hands as she set aside her book.

Evelyn sighed, setting aside the leather-bound volume she'd been reading. "I suppose we do, dear. I've been expecting this conversation for some time now."

Cat settled into the chair opposite her grandmother, feeling the weight of generations of family history pressing down upon her. "I visited Carlisle's Antiques today. Mr. Carlisle told me some things about Grandpa James and his involvement during the war. He seemed reluctant at first, but eventually opened up."

Evelyn's face paled slightly, but she remained composed, her fingers absently tracing the pattern on the armrest. "I see. And what exactly did Albert tell you? That old fox has always known more than he lets on."

"He said Grandpa was involved in recovering stolen art after the war. But there's more to it, isn't there? Something about a special task force and dangerous missions behind enemy lines?"

Evelyn was quiet for a long moment, her gaze fixed on the flickering flames of the candles lit on the table. The silence stretched between them, heavy with unspoken truths. Finally, she spoke, her voice barely above a whisper. "Your grandfather was a good man, Catalina. But sometimes, good men are forced to make difficult choices. The war... it changed everything for him, for all of us."

"What do you mean?" Cat leaned forward, her heart racing with anticipation.

"During the war, your grandfather James was part of a team tasked with recovering art stolen by the Nazis. It was dangerous work, full of close calls and moral dilemmas. But in the end, he realized that not all the recovered pieces would be safe if returned through official channels. There were powerful people on both sides who wanted to use these treasures for their own gain."

Cat leaned forward, her curiosity piqued. Her mind raced with possibilities. "So he smuggled some of the art? To keep it safe from those who might abuse its power?"

Evelyn nodded slowly, a mix of pride and sorrow in her eyes. "Yes, but not for personal gain, as far as I know. He traded and bought tons of pieces from all over the world. He held quite the collection. He believed there was something larger at stake, it was something that needed to be protected at all costs. Your grandfather carried the weight of that decision for the rest of his life."

"The Amara Necklace?" Cat ventured, her voice barely above a whisper. The name felt electric on her tongue, as if speaking it aloud might summon ancient forces.

Her grandmother's eyes widened in surprise, a flicker of fear passing across her face. "You know about that? Oh, Catalina, I had hoped to shield you from this burden for a little longer."

"I've been doing some research," Cat admitted, feeling a mix of guilt and determination. "I found some old letters and an old journal. It has a lot of cryptic writing in it. But what was so important about the necklace that Grandpa would risk everything to protect it? What power does it hold?"

Evelyn's gaze drifted to the window, her eyes unfocused, as if looking into the past. "James... he never told me the full story," she began, her voice soft with memory. "He left me his journal, and in the event if he died, it would lead me to where he kept all the antiquities he'd collected over the years. He only said that the necklace was a centerpiece of a larger collection, and that it was the key to something really big. He made me promise to keep the collection safe and never let anyone know our family had it."

Cat leaned in, hanging on every word. The weight of family secrets pressed heavily on her shoulders.

"Years after your grandfather passed," Evelyn continued, "Albert passed to me a beautiful necklace. I took the necklace and hid it in the attic until I could figure out where James kept the entire collection. After years of Albert and I trying to discover it, we basically gave up. So I left the necklace in the attic. I thought it would be safer there, away from prying eyes." She shook her head, a rueful smile on her lips. "But time has a way of playing tricks on the mind. I almost forgot where I'd put it."

Her eyes met Cat's, a mix of relief and fear swirling in their depths. "When you found it in the attic, I felt... conflicted. Relieved that it was found again, yes, but terrified that it wasn't in a safer place. I realized then how vulnerable we truly were."

Cat's mind raced with questions. "But why, Grandma? What makes this necklace so important that we need to keep it hidden?"

Evelyn sighed, her shoulders sagging under the weight of long-held secrets. "That's the thing, dear. I don't know the full extent of it. Your grandfather took many of those secrets to his grave. But from what Albert tells me, there are people out there who would stop at nothing to get their hands on it. People who believes it holds the key to something far greater than we can imagine."

Cat leaned forward, her brow furrowed. "Did you know Viktor Sterling? He seemed very interested in the necklace when I mentioned it at his gallery."

Evelyn's eyes widened, a flicker of alarm crossing her face. "You spoke to Viktor about the necklace? Oh, Catalina, that was dangerous." She took a deep breath, composing herself. "Yes, I know of Viktor Sterling. He's made several attempts over the years to find out if our family had the necklace. He's relentless, and dangerous, that one."

Cat nodded, pieces of the puzzle falling into place. "What about Albert Carlisle? How does he fit into all of this?"

Evelyn's expression softened slightly. "Albert and your grandfather James knew each other well. They became quick friends after the war, I believe. Albert became your grandfather's protégé in many ways. After James passed, I found myself at a loss. I didn't know how to handle the weight of the business he'd left behind." She paused, her gaze distant. "After he gave me the necklace, I confided in Albert about the clues in the journal, and neither of us could figure it out. He's been a godsend, really. He's helped broker art deals for the family, always keeping us one step ahead of those who might be looking for the necklace."

"So he's been helping to keep the trail cold?" Cat asked, understanding dawning on her face.

Evelyn nodded. "Exactly. Albert's connections in the art world have been invaluable. He's arranged sales of other pieces from our collection, creating a smokescreen of sorts. It's all been part of a careful dance to keep the family's name from being tarnished."

Cat leaned forward, her eyes narrowing as she processed the information. A thought nagged at her, one she couldn't shake. "Grandma," she began hesitantly, "did Grandpa James... did he bring back Nazi treasure and sell it?"

Evelyn's face flushed, her eyes darting away from Cat's intense gaze. The silence stretched between them, heavy with unspoken truths. Finally, she nodded, her voice barely above a whisper. "Yes, he did."

Cat's eyes widened, but she remained silent, waiting for her grandmother to continue.

Evelyn sighed, her shoulders sagging under the weight of the confession. "Those pieces... they had to be sold privately. It was the only way to conceal the where the items came from." She paused, her fingers twisting in her lap. "You have to understand. It was James' wish to ensure the pieces made their way back to their rightful owners. The pieces that James sold belonged to families that were no longer alive. Entire families killed in concentration camps. James made sure there were no rightful owners before selling them. He tried awfully hard and was double crossed several times. The underworld of art is shady, dear. Apparently, no one really knows who is buying what."

Cat sat back, her mind reeling from the revelation. She watched as her grandmother's eyes filled with a mix of shame and defiance.

"Your grandfather did what he thought was right," Evelyn continued, her voice stronger now. "He couldn't bear the thought of those treasures falling into the wrong hands or being lost forever. But the process of returning them... it wasn't as straightforward as he'd hoped."

Cat nodded slowly, trying to reconcile this new information with the image she'd always had of her grandfather. The weight of family secrets pressed heavily on her shoulders.

"I think... I need some time to process all of this," Cat said, rising from her chair.

Evelyn reached out, grasping Cat's hand. "I understand, dear. It's a lot to take in."

Cat made her way up to her room, her footsteps echoing through the hallway. Once inside, she closed the door and leaned against it, letting out a long breath. The room, with its familiar furnishings and childhood mementos, suddenly felt different, as if the very walls held secrets she was only beginning to uncover.

She moved to the window, gazing out at the moonlit grounds of Hawthorn Manor. The revelations of the evening swirled in her mind, each piece of information connecting to form a larger, more complex picture. Cat found herself torn between the desire to dig deeper and the fear of what else she might uncover.

As she stood there, contemplating her next move, Cat realized that the mystery of the Amara Necklace was far more intricate than she had ever imagined. The weight of her family's history, with all its complexities and moral ambiguities, rested squarely on her shoulders, and she had kicked the hornet's nest.

Chapter Nineteen

A warm wind whistled through the ancient oak trees surrounding Hawthorn Manor, their branches swaying against the inky sky. The household members and servants had retreated to the rear grounds, where they observed the Independence Day firework display bursting above the town to the south, their faces illuminated by the spectacular red, white, and blue explosions, completely unaware of the individual snaking through the darkened corridors of the now-deserted manor.

A shadowy figure moved silently through the house, a flashlight beam cutting through the darkness like a predatory eye. Dust motes danced in the narrow beam as the intruder bypassed the valuable antiques and artwork that adorned the manor's hallways - Ming vases, Renaissance paintings, and crystal decanters worth a fortune - their focus fixed on a single target: Cat's bedroom.

The door creaked open; the sound swallowed by the thick Victorian carpet. The figure moved quickly, their gloved hands sweeping across Cat's oak desk, tossing leather-bound books and carefully organized papers aside with reckless abandon. Drawers were yanked open with enough force to nearly pull them from their tracks, their contents spilled onto the floor in a chaotic mess. Clothes were pulled from the closet, wooden hangers clattering against the antique rod like hollow wind chimes.

The intruder's movements were frantic, their frustration growing with each passing moment. They ripped open Cat's backpack, scattering textbooks, notebooks, and mechanical pencils across the room like confetti. They overturned her grandmother's gifted jewelry box, its collection of childhood trinkets and costume pieces rolling across the hardwood floor like scattered marbles. But the object of their determined search remained frustratingly elusive.

The figure paused, their breath ragged in the stillness of the room, the distant boom of fireworks barely audible through the manor's thick walls. They shone the flashlight beam under the antique four-poster bed, across the wallpapered walls, searching for any sign of the hidden necklace. Their eyes settled on a small carved wooden chest, a family heirloom, tucked away in the shadowy corner.

With a grunt of anticipation, the intruder lunged for the chest, flipping open the brass-hinged lid. Inside, nestled among yellowed photographs and childhood mementos - dried flowers, old birthday cards, and tiny stuffed animals - lay a promising velvet pouch. The figure's heart pounded against their ribs as they reached for the pouch, their fingers trembling with barely contained anticipation.

But the pouch was empty, containing nothing but disappointment and stale air.

A guttural sound of rage escaped the intruder's lips as they tossed the chest aside with enough force to crack its corner, its precious contents scattering across the floor like autumn leaves. The necklace wasn't there. The figure searched the room again, their movements growing increasingly desperate and careless. They tore through Cat's belongings with mounting fury, leaving a trail of destruction in their wake that would have made a tornado proud.

Finally, defeated and empty-handed, the intruder retreated from the room, their footsteps masked by another volley of fireworks outside. They left behind a scene of utter chaos and the lingering scent of stale cigarette smoke that hung in the air like an unwelcome ghost.

Upon the festivities ending, Cat entered her room to a sight that made her heart skip several beats and her blood run cold. Her once-tidy room was a disaster zone, as if a small war had been waged within its walls. Clothes, books, and papers lay scattered everywhere like debris after a storm, with her favorite sweater torn from its hanger and crumpled in a heap by her desk. Drawers hung open at odd angles, their contents spilling onto the floor in messy heaps. Some pulled so forcefully they'd nearly come off their tracks. Her grandmother's cherished jewelry box - the antique mahogany one with delicate brass hinges that had sat proudly on her dresser for years - lay overturned, its collection of treasured trinkets scattered like fallen stars across the hardwood. Even her bed hadn't been spared, the mattress askew and her collection of decorative pillows thrown carelessly into corners.

Cat's mind raced as she took in the scene, her hands trembling slightly as she surveyed the damage in her once-pristine bedroom. Nothing of obvious value was missing - her laptop still sat undisturbed on the desk, her phone charger remained plugged in beside her nightstand, and even the small amount of cash she'd stashed in her desk drawer lay untouched beneath some old notebooks. The only thing that seemed to have been targeted was her personal space, her private sanctuary, within the historic walls of Hawthorn Manor. Whoever had done this wasn't after valuables - they were searching for something specific, methodically tearing through her belongings with an unsettling sense of purpose.

A cold knot formed in her stomach as she realized the terrible truth, her grandmother's warnings echoing in her mind like phantom whispers from the past. Someone had been searching for the Amara necklace, convinced it was hidden somewhere within the walls of her room. And they were willing to go to extreme lengths to find it - lengths that made Cat shudder as she took in the methodical destruction around her, imagining gloved hands moving through her private space with calculated precision. Whoever had done this knew exactly what they were looking for, and they wouldn't stop until they found it, no matter what damage they left in their wake.

The police arrived an hour after the 911 call from Evelyn, their cruisers casting alternating red and blue shadows across the manicured lawn. The police took detailed statements while the crime scene investigators meticulously examined Catalina's room for any evidence left behind by the intruder, photographing overturned furniture and dusting surfaces for fingerprints. Since it was only Cat's room that seemed to be the target, and the fact that numerous valuable assets throughout the house were left completely untouched, the lead investigator was visibly stumped. Questions swirled around Cat's friends, known enemies, or people she had come into contact with over the past month. Though Cat had the growing suspicion that the break-in had something to do with Viktor Sterling, she deliberately kept his name out of her answers, worried about the implications.

After two grueling hours of questions and statements, the police finally left and promised to follow up if any leads developed. The lead investigator, a weathered man with salt-and-pepper hair, recommended Evelyn keep the doors locked at all times, and set the security system active for all exterior doors, regardless of the time of day. He promised that the police would increase their roving patrols in the area for the next few days, making regular passes by the property.

"If you need anything, Mrs. Grant, please don't hesitate to call me." He passed his card to Evelyn, who took it with a shaking hand, her silver rings catching the light.

As the police team left the residence, their footsteps fading down the front walk, an oppressive quietness fell over the room. Cat began to realize the full gravity of the event and was filled with crushing regret, knowing this invasion of their sanctuary was her doing. The weight of bringing danger to her grandmother's doorstep settled heavily on her shoulders.

Chapter Twenty

Cat and Evie sat in the study of Hawthorn Manor, lit only by a few antique lamps and candles, the weight of recent events hanging heavily in the air. The ransacked bedroom had shaken them both, bringing the danger surrounding the Amara Necklace into sharp focus. The once-comforting scent of old books and polished wood now seemed tainted by the undercurrent of threat that had invaded their home. Shadows danced on the walls, cast by the flickering flames of the lit candles on the table, adding to the sense of unease that permeated the room.

"You are not to speak of this to your parents. Not until we figure out what is really going on," Evie said sternly, pointing a well-polished fingernail out towards Cat. Her voice carried an authority that Cat had rarely heard before.

"We can't keep it here anymore," Cat said, her voice barely above a whisper, as if the very walls might be listening. She glanced nervously at the windows, half-expecting to see a face peering in from the darkness outside. "It's not safe."

Evie nodded, her weathered hands clasped tightly in her lap, knuckles white with tension. The lines on her face seemed deeper than ever, etched with worry and fatigue. "You're right, dear. At this point, I don't think any of us are really safe. You've raised Viktor's suspicion with all your questions. There's no telling how far Viktor's reach extends." Her words and look of disappointment hit Cat deeply. It wasn't lost on Cat that she had re-opened a whole drama for her family, one that had been carefully buried for decades.

Cat chewed her lip, deep in thought. The ticking of the old grandfather clock in the corner seemed to echo her racing heartbeat. Suddenly, her eyes lit up with an idea, a spark of inspiration cutting through the gloom. "What if we didn't have to hide it at all? What if we could make him think he has it?"

Evie raised an eyebrow, intrigued. The faintest hint of a smile tugged at the corners of her mouth. "What do you mean?"

"A decoy," Cat explained, her words tumbling out in excitement. She leaned forward, her hands gesturing animatedly as she spoke. "We could ask Albert to create a fake necklace. Something that looks just like the real thing. If Viktor thinks he has the Amara Necklace, he'll stop looking for it, and we can keep the real one safe."

Evie's eyes widened as she considered the idea, a glimmer of hope shining through her worry. The tension in her shoulders seemed to ease slightly as she pondered the possibility. "That's... that's quite clever, Cat. Albert certainly has the skills for such a task. He's had his share of dealings with forgeries in the past, though he'd never admit it openly." She paused, her gaze drifting to the old family portrait hanging on the wall, as if seeking guidance from their ancestors. "It's risky, but it just might work. Tomorrow we will go to Albert's shop and get his opinion. In the meantime, go to bed. It's late. I've already made sure the staff is aware of the situation and we will have extra patrols around the house. So, you can sleep good. Whoever did this was a coward. They wouldn't dare try this with people in the house," Evie's voice sounded firm, but inside she wasn't so sure of anything she said.

Cat did as her grandmother asked. She ascended the stairs with the heavy guilt of opening an old family wound. She knew it was up to her to correct it, and hopefully a good night's sleep would bring some fresh ideas.

The next day, they made their way to Carlisle's Antiques, the bell above the door chiming with a familiar, comforting sound as they entered. The shop's musty scent of old books and polished wood enveloped them, a stark contrast to the tension they carried. Albert emerged from the back room, his keen eyes taking in their tense expressions, his own face growing serious. His weathered hands absently smoothed down his tweed jacket as he approached.

"Ah, the Grant ladies," he said, his voice gruff but warm, like sandpaper wrapped in velvet. "What brings you here today? You both look like you've seen a ghost." His eyes darted between them, searching for clues to their distress.

Cat glanced at Evie, who nodded encouragingly, her silver hair catching the light from the windows. "Mr. Carlisle, we need your help," Cat began, her voice steady despite the nervous energy coursing through her. Her fingers fidgeted with the hem of her hoodie as she spoke. "Someone broke into my room, searching for the necklace. We think... we think we need a decoy."

Albert's bushy eyebrows shot up, his eyes widening in surprise. The wrinkles around his eyes deepened with concern. "Oh dear! I knew this could get out of hand. My bet is one of Viktor's goons. A decoy, you say? Interesting proposition." He stroked his chin thoughtfully, already lost in the challenge of the task. His gaze became distant, as if he were mentally rifling through his vast collection of antiquities and forgeries. "It would need to be convincing enough to fool even the most discerning eye. Viktor's no amateur when it comes to art and antiquities."

"Can you do it?" Evie asked, her voice tinged with hope and desperation. She leaned forward, her delicate hands gripping the edge of Albert's cluttered desk. "Can you create something that would fool even Viktor, at least for a while? Maybe long enough to get the authorities to start asking questions?"

Albert's eyes twinkled with a mix of mischief and determination, a sly smile playing at the corners of his mouth. The challenge seemed to energize him, erasing years from his weathered face. "My dear, I've been in this business for longer than you've been alive. I've already forgotten more than you'll ever know. I've seen and handled more forgeries than I can count. If anyone can create a convincing replica of the Amara Necklace, it's me." He paused, his gaze sharpening like a hawk spotting its prey. "But," he added, his tone growing serious, "what are the plans once someone like Viktor realizes it's not the real deal? It can only fool an amateur for so long, but Viktor... it wouldn't take him but a few minutes at most to spot a fake."

"I've been thinking about that," Cat said, turning to Evie with a look that was part determination, part apology. Her brown eyes held a spark of defiance and ingenuity. "I think I have a way to clean this whole mess up. But grandma, you're not going to like it."

Albert's eyes lit up with anticipation, his earlier concern momentarily overshadowed by curiosity. He leaned in, eager to hear Cat's plan. Evelyn's shoulders slumped slightly, her face etched with extreme worry as she braced herself for what she was about to hear. The worry lines on her forehead deepened, and she clasped her hands tightly in her lap. The room seemed to hold its breath, the antique clocks ticking softly in the background, waiting for Cat to reveal her plan.

Chapter Twenty-One

Cat and Evelyn sat at the long kitchen table inspecting the beautiful yet fake necklace that Albert had spent all night creating. They ran theories of James and the Sterlings, talked about how James had passed, and finally spoke about the plan. Cat leaned in, her eyes locking onto Evie's with an intensity that spoke volumes. "Grandma, we need to work together. You know the family history, and I have the journal. We can figure this out." Her voice held a firm resolve, leaving no room for argument.

The determination in her tone was palpable, echoing through the room. Evie's gaze softened, a complex mix of pride and worry flickering across her weathered face. She nodded, a small smile playing at the corners of her mouth, her wrinkles deepening with the gesture.

Cat dashed upstairs, her footsteps echoing through the grand halls of Hawthorn Manor. The sound reverberated off the high ceilings and wood-paneled walls, a reminder of the house's age and secrets. She returned moments later, clutching the worn leather journal, its pages faded with age and secrets. The book seemed to pulse with untold stories as she spread it open on the polished mahogany table, its surface reflecting the dim light of the room. Evie leaned in to get a better look, her silver hair catching the light. Their heads bent together, one dark and one silver, they began to pour over the cryptic entries, the contrast between youth and age stark yet harmonious.

Cat's finger traced the lines, pausing at a peculiar sentence. Her nail, bitten short from nervous habit, underlined the words as she read. "Look, this one's different. 'Under the ancient guardian, where the acorn falls, the truth lies hidden.'" She looked up, her eyes shining with excitement, a spark of understanding igniting within them. "Ancient guardian—that could mean the old oak tree in the garden, right?"

Evie's brows furrowed, her eyes distant as she recalled memories from long ago. The weight of years seemed to press down on her shoulders as she spoke. "Yes, that tree has been there for centuries. Your grandfather used to call it the guardian of the estate." She paused, her gaze sharpening, focusing back on the present. "But how does that help us?"

Cat was already on her feet, her chair scraping against the floor as she stood. She grabbed a small garden spade from the corner, its metal surface dulled with use. "We need to dig beneath it. There might be something buried there." Her voice trembled with anticipation.

Evie looked dubious but stood up, brushing off her skirt with a practiced motion. "Alright, but if we find nothing but worms, don't say I didn't warn you." Her tone was light, but there was an undercurrent of tension beneath her words.

After a fruitless dig that left them both muddy and frustrated, they returned to the journal, dirt smudging its already worn pages. Cat flipped through, her frustration growing with each turn. The sound of rustling paper filled the air. Suddenly, Evie gasped, her arthritic finger pointing at a series of numbers scribbled in the margin. "Cat, these numbers—they look like a Dewey Decimal System code." Her voice quivered with sudden realization.

Cat's eyes widened, comprehension dawning on her face. "The library. We need to check the library." She was on her feet again in an instant, Evie close behind, their earlier disappointment replaced with renewed vigor. The manor's vast library loomed ahead, its heavy doors creaking open to reveal rows upon rows of dusty books, each one a silent sentinel of the past. The smell of old paper and leather enveloped them as they entered. Somewhere within its labyrinthine shelves, another piece of the puzzle awaited them, hidden among countless books and centuries of family history.

Cat and Evie entered the library, their footsteps muffled by the plush rug that lined the floor. The musty scent of old books enveloped them, a familiar and comforting smell that seemed to carry the weight of countless stories and histories. They made their way to the towering shelves, the silence of the room broken only by the distant ticking of a grandfather clock. Cat pulled out the journal, her finger tracing the series of numbers scrawled in the margin. The ink faded but still legible.

"Okay, let's see. 940.53 — that's World War II history." Cat's eyes scanned the shelves, her hand brushing along the spines of books until she found the right section. She carefully pulled out a heavy book, its cover worn with age and use, the title barely visible in faded gold letters.

Evie peered over her shoulder, her breath softly stirring the dust on the book's cover. "What's inside?" she asked, her voice a low whisper that seemed to echo in the quiet room.

Cat opened the book, her breath catching as she saw the hollowed-out center. Nestled within was an ornate brass key, its intricate design glinting in the dim light filtering through the library's tall windows. "Grandma, look!" Cat exclaimed, her voice barely above a whisper but filled with excitement.

They exchanged a glance, decades. Cat pocketed the key and continued searching the library, her eyes darting from shelf to floor to ceiling, taking in every detail of the room she thought she knew so well.

After what felt like hours of meticulous searching, they retreated back to the sitting area puzzled. Cat sat on the sprawled out on the floor while Evie flopping down on the sofa. Cat's gaze landed on a small carved rose on the floor, partially hidden beneath a rug. She remembered the phrase in the journal, 'Lies beneath the rose—'.

"There!" she pointed, coming to her knees to examine it closer. Her heart pounded in her chest, a mix of anticipation and apprehension coursing through her.

Evie's eyes widened in surprise. "I've never noticed that before," she murmured, her voice filled with wonder and a hint of unease. She watched as Cat pressed around the carving, hoping to engage something. Her granddaughter's fingers tracing the intricate carvings.

Cat pressed harder on the center of the rose and a soft click echoed through the room, and the center section of the bookcase to the far wall swung outward a few inches, revealing a dark crack that yawned before them like a doorway to the past. "Oh my," Evie whispered, her face pale as she took in the sight of the hidden entrance.

Cat pulled out her phone, switching on the flashlight and swung the bookcase fully open. The beam cut through the darkness, illuminating the first few steps of the passage. "Come on, Grandma. We've come this far," she said, her voice steady despite the hammering of her heart.

They descended into the tunnel, their footsteps echoing softly against the stone walls as the air grew cooler and damper with each step. The scent of earth and old stone filled their noses, a musty reminder of the passage's age and secrets. Shadows danced in the beam of Cat's flashlight, revealing cobwebs and the occasional scurrying insect. At the bottom of the steep staircase, they found themselves face to face with a solid oak door, its wood weathered but still formidable. An ancient-looking lock adorned its center, the metal tarnished but clearly still strong after all these years. Cat's hand trembled slightly as she retrieved the key from her pocket and inserted into the lock, her breath catching in her throat. With a deep inhale, she turned it, and a resounding click echoed through the passage, seeming to reverberate off the very foundations of the house above them. The sound hung in the air, a harbinger of revelations to come.

She slowly pushed the heavy door inward, revealing a vast underground vault that stretched out before them like a hidden world. Cat's flashlight beam swept across the room, illuminating piles of Nazi treasures that gleamed in the light. Jewelry glittered on velvet-lined trays, rare coins, and shelves straining under the weight of leather-bound books and mysterious artifacts. Each item seemed to hold a story, a piece of history that had been locked away for far too long.

Evie gasped, her hand flying to her mouth as she took in the sight. "I had no idea... all this... here, beneath our feet," she whispered, her voice filled with shock and disbelief. She looked at Cat, her eyes reflecting the glint of gold and the shadows of the past.

Cat stood frozen, her mind reeling at the implications of their discovery. The secrets of her family's past lay before her, each item in the vault a piece of a puzzle she was only beginning to understand.

Cat and Evie moved cautiously through the vault, their footsteps echoing in the cavernous space. The beam of Cat's flashlight danced across the treasures, revealing intricate details of each artifact. Evie's hand trembled as she reached out to touch a delicate porcelain vase, its surface adorned with vibrant scenes of pastoral life.

"I can't believe this has been here all along," Evie murmured, her voice barely above a whisper. "Your grandfather... he never told me about this." Sounding conflicted between joy and betrayal.

Cat nodded, her eyes wide as she took in the scope of the hidden collection. "It's incredible, Grandma. But why keep it secret for so long?"

Evie shook her head, her expression a mix of awe and concern. "I don't know, dear. But I'm sure James had his reasons."

Evie was able to find the old light switch and a single pendant light in the center of the vault came to life. Still using the light of her phone, she explored further, until her light fell upon a familiar shape. "Look," she said, pointing to a small wooden box tucked away on a shelf. "That looks just like the box the necklace was in when I was doing research." She opened it to see where a necklace was once housed.

Evie's brow furrowed. "You think it is the original box that held the necklace?"

Cat nodded, a plan forming in her mind. "Grandma, I think we need to see if it fits. I'm going to get the necklace from the attic."

"Be careful, Cat," Evie warned, her eyes darting nervously around the vault. "And hurry back."

Cat made her way back through the hidden passage and up to the library, her footsteps echoing softly in the confined space. She moved swiftly through the house, her heart pounding with each step, the weight of their discovery pressing heavily on her mind. As she climbed the creaking stairs to the attic, she couldn't shake the unsettling feeling that they were more vulnerable now than ever before, exposed to dangers they had yet to fully comprehend.

The attic was dark and musty, filled with the familiar shapes of old furniture and boxes, their outlines barely visible in the dim light filtering through the dusty windows. She reached for the overhead light and turned it on. Cat's eyes adjusted to the brightness as she carefully navigated around the cluttered space, her senses on high alert. She located the hiding spot where her grandmother had stashed the necklace earlier, her fingers brushing against various objects until they found their target. Her hand closed around the cool metal of the pendant, and she felt a strange thrill run through her, a mixture of excitement and apprehension coursing through her veins as she held the key to her family's mysteries. She placed in the opposite pocket from where she placed Albert's knockoff necklace. Just then, the lights went out.

Chapter Twenty-Two

As Cat come down from the attic, the house was dark. She reached for the light switch in the hallway and nothing happened. It wasn't just the attic light that went out, the whole house went dark. Cat made her way back downstairs and into the darkened library. Her eyes adjusting to the dim light coming through the windows. As she descended the hidden staircase, she managed to use the flashlight on her phone to navigate, her heart racing knowing that something was wrong. She kept one hand on the Amara Necklace which felt heavy in her pocket, while she used the other hand to hold her phone now being used as a flashlight. She ran through the house and into the library. As she reached the bottom of the vault stairs, she froze.

Viktor Sterling stood in the center of the vault, his cold eyes fixed on Cat. One arm was wrapped around Evie's shoulders, the other holding a gun to her temple. Evie's face was pale, her eyes wide with fear.

"Ah, Cat. So nice to see you again." Viktor's voice dripped with false charm. "I believe you have something that belongs to me."

Cat's mind raced, her body rigid with shock. How had he found them? How long had he been here? She had an instant fleeting thought: There goes the plan!

"I don't know what you're talking about," Cat said, her voice steadier than she felt.

Viktor's smile tightened. "Come now, let's not play games. The necklace, if you please. Unless you'd like your grandmother to suffer the consequences of your stubbornness."

Evie's eyes met Cat's, silently pleading. Cat's hand moved to her pocket, feeling the cool metal of the necklace against her fingertips.

"Alright," Cat said, forcing her voice to remain calm. "You win. I'll give you the necklace. Just let her go."

She slowly pulled the necklace from her pocket, holding it up for Viktor to see. His eyes gleamed with triumph, but Cat's mind was already working, piecing together a plan.

"That's a good girl," Viktor said, his grip on Evie loosening slightly. "Now, bring it to me. Slowly."

Cat took a step forward, her eyes darting around the darkened vault. She needed a distraction, something to catch Viktor off guard. As she moved closer, she began to formulate a plan, her mind racing through possibilities.

Cat's mind raced as she took another step toward Viktor and Evie. Her eyes darted around the vault, searching for anything she could use to her advantage. The room was filled with artifacts and treasures, each one a potential weapon or distraction.

As she moved closer, Cat's gaze landed on a heavy bronze statue perched on a nearby pedestal. It was within arm's reach, and she knew it could be her only chance.

"That's it," Viktor coaxed, his attention fixed on the necklace dangling from Cat's hand. "Just a few more steps."

Cat took another step, her free hand inching closer to the statue. She could see Evie's eyes widening, realizing Cat was about to do something.

In one swift motion, Cat hurled the necklace high into the air. Viktor's gaze instinctively followed its arc, his grip on Evie loosening for a split second. It was all the time Cat needed.

She grabbed the bronze statue and swung it with all her might, aiming for Viktor's gun hand. The impact was jarring, sending shockwaves up her arm. Viktor's gun and flashlight clattered to the floor as he let out a howl of pain.

Evie wrenched herself free, stumbling toward Cat. "Run!" Cat shouted, pushing her grandmother toward the stairs.

Viktor lunged for the gun, his face contorted with rage. Cat kicked it away, sending it skittering across the vault floor. She turned to flee, but Viktor's hand closed around her ankle, yanking her off balance.

Cat hit the ground hard, the wind knocked out of her. She twisted, trying to break free from Viktor's grip. Her hand closed around something cold and metallic—an ornate candlestick that had fallen from a nearby shelf.

Without hesitation, Cat swung the candlestick, connecting with Viktor's temple. He reeled back, momentarily stunned. Cat scrambled to her feet, her heart pounding in her ears.

She sprinted for the stairs, taking them two at a time. Behind her, she could hear Viktor's angry shouts echoing off the vault walls.

Viktor picked up his flashlight and scanned the vault floor frantically, his eyes darting from one glittering object to another. The necklace had to be here somewhere. He ignored the throbbing pain in his temple where Cat had struck him, focusing solely on finding his prize.

"Where are you?" he muttered through gritted teeth, pushing aside priceless artifacts with reckless abandon. He had found his gun, but the necklace was alluding him until a glint of blue caught his eye. There, half-hidden beneath a fallen tapestry, lay the Amara Necklace. Viktor snatched it up, a triumphant smile spreading across his face as he examined the sapphire pendant.

Meanwhile, Cat reached the top of the stairs, her breath shallow from fear and exertion. She spun around, grabbing the bookcase that led to the vault.

"Come on, come on," she panted, throwing her weight against it.

The bookcase groaned, stopping short from closing. Cat could hear Viktor's footsteps echoing from below, stumbling, growing louder with each passing second as he ascended the vault stairs. She pushed harder, her muscles straining with the effort.

No matter hard she pushed, the door wasn't closing. Cat's heart sank as she realized it was stuck, leaving a gap just wide enough for someone to slip through.

"No, no, no," she muttered, frantically examining the door's edge. Something was jammed in the track, preventing it from closing completely.

Cat glanced down the stairs, hearing Viktor's approach. She had mere seconds, at most, before he reached the top. Desperately, she wedged her fingers into the gap, trying to dislodge whatever was blocking the door.

Her fingertips brushed against something hard and metallic. A coin, perhaps, or a small piece of debris. Cat strained, stretching her arm as far as she could, trying to reach the obstruction.

Cat's fingers fumbled with the obstruction, her heart pounding in her ears. The sound of Viktor's footsteps grew louder, echoing up the stairwell.

"Cat, we have to go!" Evie hissed, as Cat abandoned her efforts to close the door. She grabbed Cat's arm, pulling her away from the vault entrance.

Cat stumbled, her eyes wide with fear. "But the necklace—"

"No time," Evie cut her off, half-dragging Cat across the library floor.

They raced between towering bookshelves. Cat's mind whirled, searching for an escape route. The main entrance was too far, and Viktor would surely catch them before they reached it.

Behind them, Viktor burst through the bookcase door, the Amara Necklace clutched in his fist. His eyes gleamed with triumph as he scanned the room.

"You can't hide from me!" he shouted, his voice bouncing off the library's high ceiling.

Cat spotted the service door, partially hidden behind a heavy curtain. She tugged Evie towards it, praying it wasn't locked.

Viktor's footsteps quickened, growing louder with each passing second. Cat could almost feel his breath on the back of her neck as she reached for the door handle.

The knob turned. Cat nearly sobbed with relief as she shoved the door open, pushing Evie through before following herself.

They emerged into a narrow hallway the staff used to transverse between the library and the kitchen. Cat slammed the door shut behind them and locked it, hearing Viktor curse on the other side.

"This way," Evie whispered, leading Cat down the corridor.

Behind them, they heard the library door crash open. Viktor's footsteps pounded against the hardwood floor as he gave chase.

But Viktor, realizing he had what he came for, suddenly changed course. His plan to leave no loose ends had failed, thanks to Cat's quick thinking. Viktor knew he could use his power to hinder any investigation. The sound of his footsteps faded as he veered away, heading towards the back of the library where a door to the backyard patio stood.

Cat and Evie didn't stop to press their luck. They ran on, Evie's ragged breath echoing in the empty hallway.

As they reached the end of the corridor, they entered the kitchen and locked the door behind them. Then they heard a distant door slam shut. Viktor had escaped through the library's back entrance, taking the Amara Necklace with him.

Cat's hands shook as she dialed 911, her voice trembling as she reported the break-in and theft. Evie sat nearby, her face pale and drawn, eyes fixed on the window as if expecting Viktor to reappear at any moment.

"They're on their way," Cat said, ending the call. She slumped against the wall, exhaustion washing over her. "What do we do now?"

Evie shook her head, her voice barely above a whisper. "We wait, dear. And pray."

Meanwhile, deep in the dense, shadowy woods surrounding Hawthorn Manor, Viktor paused to catch his breath, his chest heaving with exertion. His heart raced with a potent mixture of exhilaration and anticipation as he carefully pulled the Amara Necklace from his pocket, cradling it in his palm. Pale moonlight filtered through the bare branches overhead, catching on the sapphire's multitude of facets and casting an ethereal blue glow across his features.

"Finally," he murmured, a triumphant smile spreading slowly across his face. "After all these years..."

But as he examined the necklace more closely, turning it over in his hands, his smile faltered and then vanished entirely. Something wasn't right. The weight felt off, too light in his grasp, and the gold seemed oddly dull, lacking the rich luster he'd expected. Frowning, he squinted and brought the pendant closer to his eyes, scrutinizing every detail in the dim light.

Realization dawned, followed swiftly by a surge of white-hot rage that threatened to consume him. The sapphire was nothing more than cheap glass, it's cut mediocre at best, and the gold was merely a thin plating over base metal. This wasn't the priceless Amara Necklace he'd pursued for so long—it was a crude, worthless fake. Viktor's fingers clenched around the counterfeit, his knuckles turning white as he struggled to contain his fury.

Viktor's face contorted with fury. He'd been tricked, outsmarted by a teenager and an old woman.

"No," he snarled, spinning on his heel. "No!"

Without a second thought, Viktor charged back towards the manor. His earlier caution abandoned, he crashed through the underbrush, branches whipping at his face and arms. He didn't care about the noise he made or the trail he left behind. All that mattered was getting back to that vault and finding the real necklace.

Viktor made his way back through the outside entrance and kicked open the kitchen door, his face cringed with rage. The sudden crash of a splintering door frame sent Evie and Cat jumping to their feet, their hearts pounding in their chests.

"Where is it?" Viktor snarled as he raised his gun to them, his eyes wild as they darted between the two women. Sweat glistened on his forehead, and his once-immaculate suit was now torn and dirty from his mad dash through the woods.

Cat stepped in front of her grandmother, her hands raised in a placating gesture. "Mr. Sterling, please calm down—"

"Don't tell me to calm down!" Viktor roared, advancing towards them. "You think you can outsmart me with some cheap replica? Where's the real necklace?"

Evie gripped Cat's arm, her fingers trembling. Cat could feel her grandmother's fear radiating off her in waves.

"Evie, stay in the kitchen," Cat said, her voice low and urgent. She kept her eyes fixed on Viktor, watching his every move. "Now."

"But—" Evie began to protest.

"Stay!" Cat insisted, giving her grandmother a gentle push towards the kitchen table.

Evie hesitated for a moment before nodding and sitting down in the first seat she came to. Viktor made no move to stop her. She was no threat. His attention focused solely on Cat.

Cat took a deep breath, her mind racing as she tried to stay calm under Viktor's intense glare. She knew she had to buy time to keep him distracted until help arrived.

"The real necklace is in the study," she said, her voice steadier than she felt. "I can show you where it is."

Viktor's eyes narrowed, suspicion warring with desperation on his face. After a moment, he jerked his head towards the door.

"Lead the way," he growled, gesturing with his gun. "No more games... and don't try anything clever. Hands where I can see them." He quickly glanced at his Rolex watch. He knew his time was limited. He had no doubt they had dialed 911.

Cat slowly raised her hands, palms out, and began walking towards the study. Viktor followed close behind, his footsteps heavy on the hardwood floor. The barrel of the gun pressed against her back, a constant reminder of the danger she was in.

As they moved through the hallway, Cat's mind whirled with possibilities. She knew there was no necklace in the study, but she hoped that help was waiting and the police would arrive quickly.

The walk to the study felt endless, each step measured and tense. Cat could hear Viktor's ragged breathing behind her, could almost feel the waves of anger and frustration radiating off him. She kept her movements slow and deliberate, not wanting to startle him into doing something rash.

When they reached the study door, Cat paused, her hand hovering over the doorknob.

"Open it," Viktor commanded, pressing the gun harder against her back.

Cat's hand trembled as she turned the doorknob, pushing the study door open. Darkness engulfed them, the room a black void save for a sliver of moonlight peeking through the curtains.

Viktor's breath was hot on her neck as he reached around her, shining his flashlight ahead. In that split second, Cat saw her chance.

She smacked the flashlight out of his hand as she bolted into the pitch black room. She heard the flashlight hit the floor and come apart. Now the only light visible was the moonlight shining through the half opened curtains that covered the large windows.

Her feet barely touched the ground as she lunged forward into the blackness. Her inner mind drawing a picture of where the furniture and walls were. Her heart pounded in her ears, drowning out Viktor's surprised curse behind her. Cat reach the inner left wall, her outstretched hands found the familiar outline of the pocket door, left slightly ajar.

Without hesitation, she slipped through the opening, her shoulder barely grazing the wooden frame as she silently squeezed past.

The sudden darkness left Viktor disorientated. He blinked rapidly, his gun hand swinging wildly as he moved forward blindly. The girl had vanished like a ghost into the darkness, there one moment and gone the next.

"No!" Viktor snarled, his composure cracking. He charged into the room as his eyes adjusted, his eyes darting frantically from corner to corner. But Cat was nowhere to be seen. Then he saw it. Barely visible in the dark, a wooden pocket door slightly open on his left.

Chapter Twenty-Three

Cat raced down the shadowy corridor, her breath ragged as she heard Viktor's determined footsteps behind her. Her heart pounded in her chest, each beat echoing in her ears as she pushed herself to run faster. The old manor's floorboards creaked beneath her feet, betraying her position with every step.

She darted around a corner, her hand grazing the wall to keep her balance. The darkness pressed in around her, broken only by slivers of moonlight seeping through gaps in the drapes. Cat's eyes strained to make out obstacles in her path, her mind racing to recall the layout of this seldom-used wing of the house.

Viktor's angry shouts reverberated through the hallway, growing closer with each passing second. "You can't hide forever, girl!" he bellowed, his voice laced with fury and frustration.

Cat's lungs burned as she pushed herself harder, desperately searching for a way out. She spotted a narrow staircase leading down and took it without hesitation, her feet barely touching each step as she descended. The stairs groaned under her weight, and she winced at the noise, knowing it would guide Viktor straight to her.

At the bottom of the stairs, Cat found herself in a dimly lit storage area. Dusty shapes loomed in the shadows—old furniture and outdoor furniture piled high. She weaved between the obstacles, her eyes darting back and forth, seeking any potential hiding spot or escape route.

The sound of Viktor's heavy footfalls on the stairs above spurred her on. Cat ducked behind a large armoire, pressing herself against the wall. She held her breath, trying to quiet her gasping lungs as she listened intently.

Viktor's steps slowed as he reached the bottom of the stairs. Cat could hear him moving through the room, his breathing harsh and uneven. She closed her eyes, willing herself to become invisible as she heard him draw nearer to her hiding spot.

Cat ducked around the old furniture, her hand brushing against the cold stone walls as she navigated the darkness. The dust being stirred in her wake filled her nose, and she suppressed a cough, afraid the sound might betray her location. Her fingers trailed along the rough surface, guiding her forward as her eyes struggled to adjust to the nearly pitch-black surroundings.

The wall twisted and turned, leading her deeper into the bowels of Hawthorn Manor storage. Cat's heart raced, each beat echoing in the confined space. She strained her ears, listening for any sign of pursuit. Viktor's muffled curses reached her, growing fainter as she put more distance between them.

Cat's shin caught a protruding furniture leg, and she stumbled, barely catching herself before she fell. She paused, taking a deep breath to steady her nerves. The air grew cooler as she pressed on, and a faint draft tickled her skin, hinting at another opening ahead.

As she rounded a corner, a sliver of moonlight pierced the darkness. Cat quickened her pace, hope surging through her. The passage widened, opening into a small mechanical room that housed the manor's utilities. Moonbeams filtered through two narrow rectangle windows high above, casting shadows on the walls.

Cat's eyes darted around the room, searching for another exit. Ancient shelves lined old paint buckets and tools. She spotted a door on the far side, its wood beaten with age.

Viktor's voice boomed through the basement of the manor, his words dripping with venom. "Come out, come out, wherever you are, little Cat," he called, his tone mockingly playful. "You can't hide forever, and when I find you, you'll wish you had never started this little game."

Cat's breath caught in her throat as she pressed herself against the cold stone wall of the utility chamber. Her heart pounded so loudly she feared Viktor might hear it echoing through the passages.

"Do you think this is a game, girl?" Viktor's voice grew harsher, bouncing off the walls and seeping into every crevice of the old house. "I've spent decades searching for that necklace. You have no idea what you're dealing with." His slight Russian accent was stronger than before.

Cat's mind raced, trying to formulate a plan. She knew she couldn't stay hidden forever, but facing Viktor seemed impossible. Her eyes darted around the room, searching for anything she could use as a weapon or distraction.

"Your grandfather thought he could outsmart us too," Viktor continued, his footsteps growing closer. "Look where that got him. Do you want to end up the same way?"

A chill ran down Cat's spine at the implied threat. She hadn't known the full extent of her family's involvement with Viktor, but his words painted a grim picture.

"I'll tear this place apart brick by brick if I have to," Viktor shouted, his patience clearly wearing thin. "You're only prolonging the inevitable, Cat. Give me the necklace, and maybe I'll let you and your grandmother walk away from this alive."

Cat's fists clenched at the mention of Evie. She hoped her grandmother had managed to get to safety, but the uncertainty gnawed at her. She couldn't risk Viktor finding Evie, no matter what happened to her.

"Last chance, Cat," Viktor's voice echoed, closer than ever. "Come out now, or things are going to get very unpleasant for you and everyone you care about."

Cat quietly as possible opened the old door and emerged from the utility room into the square room, her eyes darting frantically around the space. The light spilled through tall, arched windows, half lighting the room. Her heart raced as she scanned her surroundings, desperately seeking her next escape route. She knew she was running out of spaces to hide.

The room appeared to be an old office or repairman's shop, long abandoned. Empty bookshelves lined the walls. What few items were there were hidden beneath layers of cobwebs and time. A massive metal desk dominated the center of the room, its surface cluttered with rags and tarnished brass instruments.

Cat's breath came in short, sharp gasps as she tried to quiet her panting. She strained her ears, listening for any sign of Viktor's approach. The old manor creaked and groaned around her, each sound amplified in the stillness of the night.

Suddenly, Viktor's voice boomed through the utility room, much closer than before. "I can hear you scurrying around like a frightened mouse, Catalina," he called out, his words dripping with malice. "There's nowhere left to run."

Panic surged through Cat's veins as she realized how close he was. Her eyes landed on another open door on the far side of the room, a sliver of darkness beckoning beyond it. Without hesitation, she dashed towards it, sprinting across the moonlit floor.

She reached the door, her fingers wrapping around the cold metal handle. With a swift tug, she pulled it open wider, revealing a now lit hallway. A staff member had found the cause of the power outage and flipped the main breaker back on. Viktor, seeing the light shine through the now open door, made his way directly

As Cat rounded the corner, her heart leaped into her throat. She nearly collided with a man emerging suddenly from an alcove. Her eyes widened in recognition as she realized it was Albert Carlisle.

The old antique dealer's face was etched with concern, his eyes darting between Cat and the door behind her. He raised a finger to his lips, signaling for silence. Cat nodded, her chest heaving as she tried to catch her breath.

Albert leaned in close, his voice barely above a whisper. "Keep running, Cat. I'll try to stop Viktor."

Cat opened her mouth to protest, but Albert shook his head firmly. He gestured urgently down the hallway, indicating she should continue her escape. The sound of heavy footsteps echoed from the direction Cat had come, growing louder with each passing second.

Albert's eyes narrowed with determination. He gave Cat a gentle push, urging her onward. "Go, now!" he hissed.

Cat hesitated for a split second, torn between her desire to help Albert and her instinct for self-preservation. The old man's steely gaze demanded no reply. With a quick nod of gratitude, Cat turned and sprinted down the corridor, her footsteps muffled by the thick center rug.

As she ran, Cat heard Albert's voice behind her, loud and clear. "Viktor! What brings you to this part of the house at such an hour?" The sound of a struggle ensued.

Cat didn't dare look back. She focused on the path ahead, her mind racing as she considered her next move.

Albert's unexpected appearance had given her a chance, and she was determined not to waste it.

The sound of raised voices echoed behind her, growing fainter as she put distance between herself and the confrontation. Cat's breath came in ragged gasps as she pushed herself to run faster, her legs burning with exertion.

Suddenly, a loud crash reverberated through the hallway. Cat stumbled, nearly losing her footing as she whipped her head around. The noise was followed by the unmistakable sounds of a fight—grunts, thuds, and the sharp crack of a walking stick breaking in half.

Cat's stomach twisted with guilt and fear. She slowed her pace, torn between continuing her escape and going back to help Albert. The muffled sounds of the fight grew more intense, spurring her indecision.

Just as she was about to turn back, Albert's words echoed in her mind: "Keep running, Cat." With a pang of regret, she forced herself to face forward and press on. Whatever was happening behind her, Albert had given her this chance to escape, and she couldn't let his sacrifice be in vain.

Cat's feet pounded against the floor as she raced down the hallway, her chest heaving with each labored breath. The old manor's walls seemed to close in around her, the shadows stretching and twisting in the dim light. She pushed herself harder, desperate to put as much distance as possible between herself and Viktor.

As she raced up the stairs, suddenly, a loud gunshot echoed through the manor, the sound reverberating off the walls and sending a chill down Cat's spine. She stumbled, her hand reaching out to steady herself against the faded wallpaper. The noise was followed by Viktor's venomous language towards Albert, a cruel and triumphant sound that made Cat's blood run cold.

"Did you really think that old fool could stop me?" Viktor's voice boomed, his words dripping with disdain.

Cat's heart sank, a wave of guilt and fear washing over her. She realized with growing horror that Albert had been no match for Viktor's strength and determination. The old antique dealer, who had appeared like a guardian angel in her moment of need, had fallen victim to Viktor's ruthlessness.

She leaned against the wall, her legs trembling beneath her. The weight of Albert's sacrifice pressed down on her, making it hard to breathe. Cat closed her eyes, fighting back tears as she imagined what might have happened to the kind old man who had tried to protect her.

Viktor's footsteps echoed through the hallway once more, growing louder with each passing second as he methodically checked every nook and cranny. Cat knew she couldn't afford to waste the precious time Albert had bought her. With a deep breath, she pushed off from the wall, forcing her tired legs to carry her forward.

The gunshot replayed in her mind, each echo bringing with it a fresh wave of horror. Albert's anguished cry that followed, a sound that would haunt Cat for years to come. The guilt crashed over Cat like a tidal wave. Her legs trembled beneath her, threatening to give way as the full weight of what had happened settled on her shoulders.

Cat's mind raced, grappling with the reality of the situation. Viktor had proven just how far he was willing to go to get what he wanted. The sound of the gunshot had shattered any illusions Cat might have had about the stakes of this deadly game. This wasn't just about a necklace anymore — it was about survival.

Viktor's voice rang out, closer now, sending a chill down Cat's spine. "Your friend Albert can't help you anymore, little Cat," he called, his tone dripping with malice. "It's just you and me now. Why don't you make this easier on yourself and come out?"

For a moment, despair threatened to overwhelm her. But as Viktor's footsteps echoed through the hallway, growing ever closer, a surge of adrenaline coursed through Cat's veins. She couldn't let Albert's sacrifice be in vain. She had to keep going. She had to at least keep stalling until the police arrived. That was her only hope now.

With renewed desperation, Cat pushed herself. Her legs were weak with exertion, but she ignored the pain, focusing solely on putting as much distance between herself and Viktor as possible. The old manor's corridors, hallways, and its many rooms seemed to stretch endlessly before her, each turn revealing another direction.

Cat's mind raced as she ran, trying to recall the layout of Hawthorn Manor. She had explored these halls countless times as a child, but now, under the weight of fear, everything seemed unfamiliar.

Viktor continued to taunt her. His words only spurred Cat to greater anxiety. She knew he was right—she couldn't keep running forever. But she didn't need forever. She just needed enough time for the police to arrive.

Cat was out of places to hide. She had circled the house until she was back at the library. Her thoughts ran to locking herself in the vault, but that would leave Evie alone. Viktor would have no issue using her to get his way.

Cat stepped into the middle of the library, seemingly to give up just as Viktor turned the corner of the library entrance. He had her this time.

"Where is it?" Viktor demanded, his patience wearing thin. "Where's the Amara Necklace?"

Cat stood in utter silence before him, looking frightened, out of options, and out of time. She steady her mind in knowing this was the end.

"Enough games, Catalina," he growled as he slowly stepped forward, his voice low and menacing. "Where's the necklace?"

Cat stood her ground, chin lifted in defiance. She fought to keep her voice steady as she replied, "Why should I tell you anything? You're nothing but a thief and a murderer."

Viktor's lips curled into a sneer as he slapped her with his free hand. "Oh, that's rich coming from you. Your family's been sitting on stolen goods for decades. You're no better than me."

"We're nothing alike," Cat shot back, her hands clutching her cheek. "My grandfather was trying to protect these things, not hoard them like some dragon."

Viktor took a step even closer, looming over Cat. "Protection? Is that what you call it? Wake up, girl. Your precious grandfather was a thief, just like the rest of us."

Cat felt anger bubbling up inside her, hot and fierce. "You don't know anything about my family or what they've been through!"

"I know more than you think," Viktor sneered. His hand shot out, gripping Cat's arm tightly. "Now, where is the Amara Necklace? Don't.. make.. me.. ask.. again."

Viktor's eyes flashed dangerously. "You have no idea what I'm capable of. I've spent a long time waiting for that necklace, and I won't let some stubborn teenager stand in my way."

"Maybe that's your problem," Cat retorted, twisting her arm free. "You're so obsessed with the past that you can't see what's right in front of you."

Viktor's eyes narrowed as he glared down at Cat, his gaze suddenly drawn to a glint of gold on her throat. His breath caught as realization dawned.

"You little snake," he hissed, a mixture of fury and triumph flashing across his face. "It's been right there all along."

Cat's hand instinctively flew to her neck, but it was too late. Viktor's arm shot out, his fingers wrapping around the delicate chain of the Amara Necklace. With a sharp yank, he tore it from her neck, the back clasp snapping under the force.

"No!" Cat cried out, reaching for the necklace as it dangled from Viktor's grasp.

Viktor's lips curled into a cruel smile as he held the necklace up to the dim light, admiring its glittering sapphire. "Finally," he breathed, his voice thick with satisfaction.

But his moment of triumph was short-lived. A dull thud echoed through the library, and Viktor's eyes widened in shock. The necklace slipped from his fingers as he fell to his knees, revealing Albert Carlisle standing behind him, a heavy antique candlestick gripped tightly in his weathered hands.

"I believe," Albert said, his voice steady despite the gravity of the situation, "that doesn't belong to you, Mr. Sterling."

Chapter Twenty-Four

"You're bleeding!" Cat cried as she noticed Albert's leg covered in blood from the thigh down.

"Never mind that, quickly now," Albert huffed, his face red with exertion. "We need to seal the vault before the police arrive." His words came out in short bursts, his breath labored from the exertion.. at rushed to the vault bookcase door, her fingers fumbling for what blocked its closure. Sweat beaded on her forehead as she worked, her heart pounding in her chest. She found the culprit and removed it from the track. With a satisfying click, the passage sealed itself, the carved rose panel blending seamlessly into the floor once more, erasing any evidence of their clandestine activities.

Albert did his best to tie Viktor's hands and feet with a long tassel he ripped from the curtains.. just as they were finishing, the sound of sirens pierced the air. Cat's heart raced as she heard car doors slamming outside.

"Perfect timing," Albert muttered, straightening his jacket. His eyes darted around the room, ensuring everything was in place.

Viktor began to stir, a low groan escaping his lips. His eyes fluttered open, confusion evident on his face as he took in his surroundings. He blinked rapidly, trying to piece together what had happened after being concussed.

Evie was already at the entrance with the door open, pointing and directing the police towards the library.. our police officers entered and made their way swiftly to the library, their hands on their holsters. Their boots echoed on the hardwood floors, adding to the tension in the air. "What's going on here?" the lead officer demanded, eyes darting between Cat, Albert, and the dazed Viktor on the floor. His voice was authoritative, cutting through the chaos of the moment.

Albert calmly sat in a large reading chair, his demeanor a stark contrast to the frenetic energy around him. "Well, for starters, this man shot me!" he announced, gesturing towards his leg. The officers' gazes immediately dropped to his pant leg, now soaked in blood, the dark stain a stark testament to the violence that had occurred.

Cat took a deep breath, steeling herself for what was to come. She advanced, her tone more composed than her inner turmoil suggested. "This individual," she gestured toward Viktor, who was now struggling to sit up, "forcibly entered our home and stole a priceless family heirloom. He wounded Mr. Carlisle during the robbery and kept us at gunpoint until we managed to overpower him." Her voice trembled slightly, but she kept her chin high, meeting the officer's gaze steadily.

Viktor struggled to sit up, his eyes now fully alert and filled with fury. His usually impeccable appearance was disheveled, his silver hair mussed and his suit wrinkled. "That's preposterous! I-" he began, his voice rising with indignation.

"The necklace is in his jacket pocket," Cat interrupted, her gaze locked with the officer's. "You can check for yourself." She stood her ground, refusing to be intimidated by Viktor's glare.

The second officer moved towards Viktor, who tried to scoot away, his movements still sluggish from his recent unconsciousness. "Now wait just a minute-" Viktor protested, his voice laced with panic.

But it was too late. The officer reached into Viktor's pocket and pulled out the Amara Necklace, its sapphire glinting in the light. The room fell silent for a moment as everyone stared at the beautiful piece of jewelry, its presence damning evidence against Viktor.

Viktor's face paled as he realized Cat had planted it on him while he was knocked out.. is mind racing to the gravity of his situation. The color drained from his cheeks, leaving him looking ghostly in the library's warm lighting. He glared at Cat, his voice a low, menacing whisper. "You'll regret this!" His eyes burned with a mixture of anger and defeat.

As the officers stood Viktor up, they were already reading him his rights. The familiar words echoing in the old library, Cat felt a wave of relief wash over her. The tension in her shoulders began to ease, and she allowed herself a small, triumphant smile. She glanced at Albert, who gave her a wink and a subtle nod of approval. In that moment, Cat knew that despite the challenges they had faced, they had emerged victorious... but more importantly, alive.

Chapter Twenty-Five

The officers moved swiftly, their practiced hands securing the handcuffs around Viktor's wrists. The cold metal clicked into place, echoing in the now-silent library. Viktor's face contorted with a mixture of rage and disbelief as the reality of his situation was truly sinking in.

"Viktor Sterling, you're under arrest for attempted murder, breaking and entering, assault with a deadly weapon, and grand larceny for staters," the lead officer recited, his voice firm and unwavering. "You have the right to remain silent. Anything you say can and will be used against you in a court of law..."

As the Miranda rights continued, Viktor's shoulders slumped. The once-proud art collector now looked defeated, his carefully curated image crumbling before everyone's eyes. His gaze darted around the room, landing on the faces of those who had outsmarted him—at Albert, and even the stoic Evie.

The officers guided Viktor towards the front door, his expensive shoes scuffing against the polished hardwood floors. Each step seemed to drain more of his composure. As they passed through the grand foyer, Viktor's eyes lingered on the paintings and artifacts that adorned the walls–pieces similar to those he had coveted for so long.

Outside, the flashing lights of police cars illuminated the night, casting eerie shadows across the manicured lawn of Hawthorn Manor. Viktor Sterling, once the toast of high society, will now be the subject of whispers and gossip.

As he was led down the steps, Viktor's thoughts turned to his father. The Sterling name, once synonymous with prestige in the art world, would now be forever tarnished. Years of carefully constructed deals, hidden acquisitions, and shadowy transactions would all come to light. The empire his father had built, and that Viktor had expanded, was crumbling around him.

The realization hit Viktor like a physical blow. His legacy, the one thing he had fought so hard to protect and enhance, was now in tatters. The weight of his defeat seemed to press down on him, causing him to stumble slightly as he approached the waiting police car.

As the police car carrying Viktor disappeared around the corner, Albert's brow furrowed with concern as the paramedic wrapped his leg. He turned to Cat, his eyes darting to the necklace in the evidence bag held by one of the remaining officers.

"I don't like this one bit," Albert muttered, his voice low enough for only Cat to hear. "Viktor's got friends in high places. That necklace might vanish into thin air before it even reaches the evidence room. If he gets the Amara Necklace, he'll have everything he needs to find that treasure trove somewhere in Germany."

Cat's eyes widened as she realized the implications of Albert's words. The Amara Necklace, with all its history and secrets, was the linchpin to untold antiquities and religious artifacts still hidden in Germany. It could be lost forever if it fell into the wrong hands.

Albert's arthritic fingers tapped nervously against his injured leg as he watched the officer carefully place the evidence bag in the trunk of his patrol car. "You don't know the kind of strings Viktor can pull, even from behind bars. He's got connections that run deeper than you can imagine."

Cat's mind raced, trying to process Albert's concerns while still reeling from the night's events. She glanced at the officer, who was now engaged in conversation with Evie, taking her statement about the break-in.

Albert leaned in closer, his voice barely above a whisper. "That necklace holds secrets that could shake the art world to its core. If it disappears now, we will never see it again. And who knows what Viktor's associates might do with that kind of power?"

Cat's eyes sparkled with mischief as she caught Albert's gaze. With a subtle movement, she reached into her pocket and pulled out the real Amara Necklace, holding it just enough out of the pocket for Albert to see before quickly tucking it away again.

Albert's eyes widened in surprise, then crinkled with amusement. He let out a low chuckle, shaking his head in admiration.

"Well, I'll be damned," he whispered, careful not to draw attention from the nearby officers. "You're a clever one, aren't you?"

Cat's lips curved into a sly smile. "I learned from the best," she murmured, nodding towards her grandmother.

Albert's shoulders relaxed, the tension visibly leaving his body. "And here I was, worrying myself sick over nothing," he said, his voice a mix of relief and pride. "You've got more of your grandfather in you than I thought."

Cat glanced around, making sure no one was watching them. The officers were still busy taking statements and cataloging evidence. Evie caught her eye from across the room and gave her a knowing nod.

"I couldn't risk losing it," Cat explained in a hushed tone. "Not after everything we've been through. The fake should keep the police busy for a while, at least."

Albert nodded approvingly. "Hey, what happened to the plan?

"He showed up a little early, but it all worked out." She said, smiling.

"Smart thinking on the switch, but what do you plan to do with the real one now?"

Cat's brow furrowed as she considered the weight of the question. The necklace in her pocket felt heavier than ever, laden with secrets and responsibilities she was only beginning to understand.

"I'm not sure yet," she admitted. "But I know we can't let it fall into the wrong hands again."

Albert placed a gentle hand on her shoulder. "Whatever you decide, you've got a good head on your shoulders. Your grandfather would be proud."

Chapter Twenty-Six

Cat and Evie sat side by side on the worn leather couch in Hawthorn Manor's living room, their eyes fixed on the evening news. The familiar jingle of the breaking news segment filled the air, and the anchor's voice cut through the silence, echoing off the antique-filled walls of the grand old house.

"In a shocking turn of events, renowned art collector Viktor Sterling has been arrested and charged with multiple crimes," the anchor announced, her tone grave and her expression serious.

Cat leaned forward, her heart racing as images of Viktor in handcuffs being escorted by FBI agents into the courthouse flashed across the screen. His usually impeccable suit was rumpled, and his silver hair disheveled. Evie reached out and squeezed her granddaughter's hand, a gesture of comfort and shared relief. The warmth of her grandmother's touch grounded Cat, reminding her that the nightmare was finally over.

The news segment continued, detailing the charges against Viktor: attempted murder, breaking and entering, assault, and theft. The anchor's voice grew more intense as she reported on the fallout from Viktor's arrest, her words painting a picture of a crumbling empire.

"But that's just the beginning of his troubles.. he Sterling Galleria, once a beacon of the art world, has been shut down pending a federal investigation," she said, her voice tinged with a hint of disbelief. "All art pieces from the gallery are scheduled to be auctioned off soon, with proceeds going to a fund for victims of art theft. Individuals that have the proper paperwork to claim any of the items, should call the FBI tip line at the number on the screen."

Cat couldn't help but feel a twinge of satisfaction as she watched footage of police tape surrounding the once-prestigious gallery. The place that had seemed so intimidating just days ago now looked small and shabby in the harsh light of day, its grand facade stripped of its mystique.

"Viktor Sterling's fall from grace has sent shockwaves through the art community," the anchor continued, her tone reflecting the gravity of the situation. "Many powerful figures who once courted his favor are now distancing themselves from the disgraced collector. Sources say that some of Sterling's former associates, upon learning of his shady deals, have expressed... less than charitable sentiments towards him."

Evie shook her head, her expression a mix of disbelief and relief. The lines on her face seemed to deepen as she absorbed the news. "I never thought I'd see the day," she murmured, her voice barely above a whisper. "He'll have to have eyes in the back of his head the rest of his life".

Cat nodded, her mind racing with the implications of Viktor's downfall. She could almost feel the ripple effects spreading outward, touching lives far beyond the art collecting community. Perhaps those who were stolen from could reclaim their heirlooms, their family histories finally restored after years of loss and uncertainty. She thought of all the other collectors like Viktor, wondering if they were watching this broadcast too, sweating in their mansions as they contemplated their own questionable acquisitions. The news segment concluded with a final shot of Viktor being led away by agents, his once-proud demeanor now replaced by a look of defeat. His perfectly tailored suit seemed to hang loose on his frame, as if his very presence had diminished. As the camera zoomed in on his face, Cat caught a glimpse of the man behind the mask–vulnerable, exposed, and utterly alone. Those piercing gray eyes that had once commanded such fear and respect now darted nervously, searching for an escape that wouldn't come.

Chapter Twenty-Seven

A month after the dramatic events surrounding Viktor Sterling's arrest, Cat stood in her room at Hawthorn Manor, surrounded by open suitcases and piles of clothes waiting to be packed. She folded a pair of well-worn jeans and placed it carefully in her bag, her mind already drifting to the upcoming senior year and the challenges that lay ahead at Riverside Academy. The familiar scent of old wood and lavender filled the air, mingling with the musty sweetness of the aged house, reminding her of countless summers spent exploring the manor's hidden corners and uncovering its character. Through her bedroom window, late afternoon sunlight streamed in, casting lines of highlights across the antique furniture and creating patterns on the plush Persian rug beneath her feet.

Cat paused, her hand hovering over a stack of books, their well-worn spines a testament to her voracious reading habits. Dog-eared pages and cracked bindings marked her favorites - mysteries and historical novels that had fueled her imagination on countless rainy afternoons. She'd miss this place, with its secrets and history, the creaking floorboards that seemed to whisper stories of the past. The ancient walls surrounding her had witnessed generations of Grant family dramas unfold, and now held her story too. But it was time to return to her normal life, or at least as normal as it could be after everything that had happened. The thought both excited and terrified her, sending a familiar flutter through her stomach as she contemplated returning to the structured world of classes and homework, where the biggest mystery was usually what would be served for lunch in the cafeteria.

Her phone buzzed on the nightstand, the screen lighting up with an incoming call. Cat's eyebrows raised as she saw Albert's name flash across the display. She hadn't heard from him in weeks, and a mixture of curiosity and apprehension filled her as she reached for the device.

"Hey Albert!" she answered, tucking a strand of hair behind her ear, her heart beating a little faster in anticipation.

Albert's voice came through, filled with barely contained excitement. "Guess what six necklaces I just bought at auction?" His words singing and carrying a hint of mischief, as if he was sharing a delicious secret.

Cat's eyes widened, her hand freezing midway through folding a t-shirt. The implication of Albert's words hit her like a thunderbolt, sending a shiver of excitement down her spine. She knew exactly what he meant, and the possibilities made her head spin.

Without a second thought, Cat began unpacking her bag. "I'll be there in an hour!"

Milton Keynes UK
Ingram Content Group UK Ltd.
UKHW051110051224
451897UK00015B/83/J